P9-DHR-344

THE THREE WOMEN K

THE THREE WOMEN K

Helke Sander

Translated by Helen Petzold

Library of Congress Catalog Card No: 90-60277

British Library Cataloguing in Publication Data
Sander, Helke
  The three women K.
    I. Title II. Die Geschichten der drei Damen K. *English*
  833.914 [F]

  ISBN 1-85242-171-1

First published 1987 as *Die Geschichten der Drei Damen K.* by Weissmann
Verlag Frauenbuchverlag GmbH, Munich. Copyright © 1987 by
Weissmann Verlag Frauenbuchverlag

This edition first published 1991 by
Serpent's Tail, 4 Blackstock Mews, London N4

Set in 10/13pt Bodoni by AKM Associates (UK) Ltd, London

Printed on acid-free paper by
Nørhaven A/S, Viborg, Denmark

CONTENTS

Foreword 7

Ms K and the Male Celebrity 9

Putting Your Money Where Your Mouth Is 13

Gratitude 17

Dr K and the Fight for Survival 19

The Birthday Guest 26

The Faith Healer 29

Talking Among Themselves 31

The Telephone Call 35

Talking Among Themselves 38

The Making of a Hero 39

Expedition With a UFO 47

Talking Among Themselves 80

A Holiday Letter 82

Ms K Watches Another Woman 92

Talking Among Themselves 101

Halloween in Berlin 105

Talking Among Themselves 116

A Telephone Conversation With a Friend 118

Talking Among Themselves 131

Four Women and a Man 134

The three Ms K spent the week between Christmas and New Year together in a village high up in the Alps. The hut, which friends had let them have for the week, was really too small for the three of them but they made the best of it. All three were successful professionally, with a tendency to hide their light under a bushel, which had its financial repercussions. They had all three recognized this tendency and fought it. The children and husbands of two of them had already left home. The third was pregnant and had been left in the lurch. Being alone had united the three — whose surnames all began with the letter K —for this particular week in this particular place. That was part of the problem that had driven each of them to the other.

During the day, one Ms K acted as a cross-country skiing instructor for the others. The other two reciprocated by cooking excellent meals. An initial visit to the village inn on Christmas Eve proved to be too expensive and too tiring. So they usually stayed in in the evenings drinking lemon verbena tea to calm their nerves. They even acquired a taste for it. But at night, when each thought the others were asleep, Ms K's soft sobbing could be heard now and then from the bedroom, or Ms K in the living room cried out in her nightmare for the man who had left her and even the third Ms K tossed to and fro in her bed, moaning. Tactfully, each of the three ladies kept to herself the secret the others had revealed.

Nevertheless, it was a distinctly merry lot that would go skiing in the mornings, then shop and cook, write letters and read. The 'three girls' soon became well-known in the village; they were under observation.

To protect themselves from the cruel nights, and to put them off for as long as possible, they began to tell each other stories in the evenings. (They had no television.) The stories had to be essentially true and should also have a funny side, those were the sole conditions.

MS K AND THE MALE CELEBRITY

Ms K felt elated. Here she was lying in bed next to a man who was celebrated for his cultural achievements. Quite anachronistically, this man had been fondling her knees and holding hands with her under the table all evening while, above it, the select gathering of people to which she had also been invited was engaged in a lively and witty discussion on cooperation in the arts. Ms K's financial circumstances were secure for the next few months and she intended to turn this situation to her advantage. She even felt she could use this time to establish herself for a few more months, if not years. Thus, she was able to join in the discussion on equal terms. She could see herself as a thread in a piece of fabric to which all those present were contributing their pattern. Later, it had so happened that Ms K, a stranger to the city in which this was taking place and who had only just arrived, found temporary accommodation with this very man. Given that the only other bed in the place was littered with books, as was the sofa, it made sense that they should be lying next to each other in his large bed.

Ms K found it nice and even amusing the way the man lay beside her, signalling discretion by stiffly keeping his distance while they said goodnight to each other. Set against the events of the evening, the gap between them was too large. To narrow it down to a distance commensurate with their feelings for each other, Ms K obligingly slid her outstretched arm under the man's head and switched off the light. The man gave a sigh of relief and turned towards her. The warmth and the smell between them were good and so it was that they first of all drew closer together and then, without changing position and almost without moving, slept together. This satisfying span of events — at the end of which a very contented Ms K, exhausted from the journey and the previous weeks' work, slipped off to sleep — was rudely interrupted and she woke up again. The man, it seemed to her, was now showing her his repertoire as a lover rather than any genuine emotion. Wide awake again now, being in a good mood and full of tender irony for this man, it wasn't difficult, it was easy for her to give her attention to their bodily entanglement and exchange of caresses and convolutions. He's rushing things too much, she thought, he could be wonderful if he were more relaxed. Oh, yes. That is what Ms K was thinking as the man whispered to her in a soft voice saying that she could count on him any time and he meant that literally. He could provide her with at least 40,000 to 50,000 Deutschmarks from a trust fund he administered for artistic projects such as hers. In fact, Ms K's artistic projects were never anything but very expensive, which was only in the nature of things. It was also the source of her frequent bitterness. But did he have to tell her this at this moment? Ms K said nothing. She was annoyed but the male celebrity protested to her all the more passionately that his offer was meant seriously and she should take him up on it. Really, any time. Strictly speaking, it was, after all, a wonderful piece of news. Why didn't she appreciate it then? He could put the offer down in writing and give it to her in the morning. Not that there's anything wrong with talking business in bed. It's just that it was the last thing that would have occurred to her at that moment.

Ms K had to return to her home town the next day. It was about 500 km away. The man was planning ahead. He wanted to see her again. Soon. When could it be? She'd no idea, said Ms K, and she meant it that way. She wasn't sure whether she wanted to see this male celebrity again so soon, even if the thought had flashed across her mind several times the previous evening that with someone like him it might at last be possible to achieve an EXCHANGE between man and woman.

— But I do want to see you again so badly, he insisted. To put an end to the matter and to show how impossible it would be for them to have a relationship, Ms K spelt out to the man just how far apart they lived. The cost of air fares was prohibitive, and car or train was out of the question. Would he please exercise his imagination and envisage what that meant.

— Oh, that's nothing, the man said. An hour. That's just a local flight. Ms K should come and visit him, it was impossible for him to get away from his work.

— I'm broke, said Ms K, relieved.

That was no problem, he could pay.

— Even if we quarrel? Ms K asked.

The male celebrity looked blank. Ms K explained, seeing at once what it was that he didn't understand.

— You would pay even if the tables were turned: if I wanted to come and you didn't want me to?

— Yes, even then, said the man.

That doesn't have to mean a thing, thought Ms K. He's only saying it because he's seen he can't pin me down. In fact, he would get round a problem like that as easy as anything if he wanted to. They went on making promises and excuses like this for quite some time, and Ms K stubbornly refused to give way to the powerful surge of love she suddenly felt for this man.

So he paid for the tickets and she reflected on love in the jet age while she flew from one city to the other to see him. After all, he had less time than she had. He had important work to do while she hadn't because she never got round to securing the finances for her, in her opinion, equally important work. It wasn't long before one of the dates they had agreed on didn't suit him, soon to be followed by another and another and so flights were succeeded by telephone communication. When Ms K pointed out that the turn of events she had anticipated now seemed to have materialized and she wanted to see him again at least once, he refused. Then — following her protest — he did visit her, only to inform her that he couldn't have one biography (as he expressed it) in city X, another in city Y and a third in city Z where he lived. The third biography was news to Ms K; she lived in the same place as the male celebrity and he married her soon after. It just seemed practical.

It had been too much. He'd been demanding too much of himself. With that he bade her a brisk farewell, leaving behind him a Ms K previously so content and composed, bellowing out her fury and disappointment and contempt at this mode of dismissal.

Two years later, when Ms K was in urgent need of money to complete a project, she remembered what this man had said, that she could count on his support any time. She mulled it over in her mind and came to the conclusion that she could accept his support now that there was nothing between them and she really wanted to do this project.

So she asked him — quite confidently, as it happened — how things stood. She did not have the courage, however, to remind him of their first night of love and his everlasting promise, it was too embarrassing. But the man refused Ms K, explaining that the fund no longer existed. There was no more money. Not long after that she heard of two projects that had recently received subsidies from this very fund. The payments had been made to women.

He was a revolutionary and a resistance fighter in the Algerian war. She was his wife and taught literacy to the liberated population. Later, after the war and back in Europe again, she supported the family — him, herself, and one child — teaching at a university in southern Germany, first on a contract basis and later with life tenure. His income was irregular. Now and then, he wrote articles on political movements in Africa. He was regularly invited to speak at left-wing political congresses and he was also interviewed on radio and, less often, on television when there was public debate on Central and South American liberation movements. From time to time, he would intervene in the latest conflicts, acting as a spokesman for struggling minorities. When, after fifteen years of marriage, they divorced, he was still able to claim under the terms of his wife's health insurance policy for a further year. During this time he had his teeth straightened and asked his former wife to advance him the money for the dental fees seeing as she would be reimbursed by the insurance company. His wife didn't have the money and anyway she'd had enough. In the end, the bills were paid by his mother, who lived in France. A few months later, the insurance company credited 950 marks to Ms K's account. By that time, she had heard that the dentist had treated him free of charge and, in a generous gesture, repaid the money he had already received — out of sympathy with the former freedom fighter (solidarity, he called it). Ms K didn't see why her husband should make a profit on his teeth on top of everything else and gave all the money to her daughter instead of sending it to his mother as originally agreed.

She wanted to give her daughter a treat and make up for something she had long felt deprived of so she told her the money was a gift from her father. The daughter was beside herself with joy for up to then her father had been uncommonly unforthcoming in so far as either his presence or gifts were concerned. He had never paid maintenance for the child and, at some point, Ms K had given up asking. She was even proud of managing everything on her own. In this way, she herself was supporting his view that as an important political personality he could not be expected to do any tedious or regular kind of work. So the daughter bought herself some clothes and rejoiced in the glorious feeling of having a father who cared for her. She talked about the generous gift wherever she went. This, in turn, embittered Ms K for what her daughter was bragging about so much was no more than she gave year in, year out, not that that was ever even mentioned. Apart from which, the loving father hadn't the slightest idea of the happiness he had given his daughter as he was, at the time, on one of the first trips by Western leftists to Albania.

Feelings of resentment, hatred and rivalry had taken such a hold of Ms K that she began psychoanalysis, which she took on an extra job to pay for. The analyst, a woman, prompted her to ask herself why she had, firstly, given the money to her daughter and not kept it for herself and why she had, secondly, concealed the whole thing from her husband.

Ms K fully intended to acknowledge her faults and mend her ways. As the money had already been spent and she could no longer take it away from her daughter and lavish it on herself, she sent her ex-husband a letter telling him the full story. She had a lively sense of humour and never ceased assuming he had one, too. So she wrote telling him that she had given their daughter a gift about which he knew nothing at all, saying it was from him. However, his daughter had been so delighted that he really ought to give it his post-facto endorsement. Ms K was unaware that she was telling him nothing new since he had shortly before received an effusive letter of thanks from his daughter which had flattered him immensely. He showed it around all over the place for it clearly stated that he gave the child generous gifts. He wrote back to Ms K immediately. This even developed into a fairly lengthy correspondence between the one-time husband and wife. Ms K was overjoyed at this for, to begin with, she believed it had now become possible to place their almost twenty-year-long relationship on a new footing. After all, they had once loved each other and she did not mean to allow paltry things to stifle an attachment of that kind. But besides expressing a similar wish on his part and referring vaguely to their joint political past, the sole purpose of his letters, which had become frequent by now, was to prove to her that she had had no right to keep the money for his teeth. He demanded it back from her so that he could, as he wrote, return it to his mother. Ms K took offence at this. She mockingly pointed out to him that he had, after all, been a father himself for seventeen years now and that also involved certain obligations. Apart from which, she knew that the debts he owed his mother could not be put down to his teeth. He finally succeeded in bringing her round to paying him the money in monthly instalments by arguing that his new girlfriend had already met a lot of his expenses and there was no way he could borrow any more money from her. On the contrary, he had to repay some of it, he wrote bitterly. Ms K did not wish to involve the other woman in complications that were still left over from his first marriage. In fact, it troubled her that another woman was so happy to take such an irresponsible man off her hands. Naturally, these guilt feelings were worked through in analysis but even so she still couldn't help feeling guilty that there he was living at the expense of a woman again.

The other woman happened to hear the story of the tooth-money by way of a remark the daughter let slip during an argument she had with her father while she was visiting him. She had already puzzled over the first woman's monthly cheques which had been trickling into her account — his being frozen — and now she too felt ashamed of the way her boyfriend had behaved. She decided to send the money she had already received back to the first woman. She had already made out the cheque when the man threw himself at her feet. He actually went down on his knees before her. He wept, he sobbed and he implored his new girlfriend not to do this to him. He begged her to save his face. But that put an end to her love for him. It just took a while for her to face up to the fact.

Another year passed and the daughter heard about this incident from the other woman with whom she had made friends. She had separated from the man by that time. He was now living with a third woman.

GRATITUDE

Ms K's business as a freelance illustrator had been going very well recently. So she decided to take out a life insurance policy for hard times to come and to provide for her old age. Her boyfriend, more experienced than she in bureaucratic matters of this nature, accompanied her to the broker, advised her on the small print and ultimately took over the proceedings. She sat gratefully betwen the two men in the office. They gave her the feeling they were negotiating the best for her. Words such as 'paragraph' or 'section' rang in her ears and formed images in her mind that combined to create delightful patterns. She watched the men making deletions and insertions and exemptions without grasping the meaning of what they were doing or what she heard. She basked in the feeling of how wonderful it was to have this man at her side taking all this off her hands. Overwhelmed, she smiled now and then at each of them quite foolishly. She was bursting with affection and named him as her heir in the event of her death.

A few years later, he left her. And soon after that, he demanded compensation for the furniture he had left behind in the flat they had shared, especially for the things in his study, the majority of which had been bought with her money. He talked about the huge sums of money invested in the flat. In particular, he mentioned the expense of the wall-to-wall carpet. Ms K ripped the carpet out and instructed a removal firm to transport the tattered, old thing they had been trampling on for the last seven years to his new address.

Not leaving it at that, she also smashed several valuable pieces of china and sent him half the fragments of each cup or plate. She even cut in half some books they had bought together. She then turned her attention to the insurance papers. She read through the provisions for the first time. They were such that her boyfriend would receive the endowment in the event of her death. Should she enjoy a long life, however, the money would be payable to her at the age of eighty-five.

Dr K AND THE FIGHT FOR SURVIVAL

In the end she told her best friend about it rather than confide in another friend who was working in a similar field as herself despite the fact that the latter would have shown more understanding of her predicament. You might say the second girl would have been better qualified to grasp the implications of the affair and all its ins and outs right from the start. And that would have been just what Ms K PhD needed. But she was afraid that this friend and colleague would get so worked up about it — and want to use the affair to settle old scores of her own — that she would not be able to keep it to herself, something Dr K even approved of in principle. But it might then have reached the ears of the person in question, with consequences possibly even more disastrous than they already were.

When Dr K asked her best friend to help her out of this mess for God's sake, she already knew she was making a great mistake careerwise. For what Dr K chose to do was to ask her best friend to accompany her to a scientific congress at which she, Dr K, was to receive an award and the considerable sum of money that went with it. The reason she asked her was because she knew that the director of the firm that was to benefit from the results of her research had no intention of missing this opportunity of going with Dr K to the other city. It had given Dr K the shock of her life to hear this. The director briefly informed her that he intended to join her in celebrating the honour that had been bestowed upon her and he would not take no for an answer. Dr K thanked him

profusely and politely expressed her appreciation of the
consideration he was showing her but drew his attention to
the amount of work he had to do and the time and trouble
these two days would cost him. Indeed, she even swallowed
her pride to the extent of dismissing the whole affair as
nothing that important any way, anything to prevent him
from going with her. But he was adamant and did not intend
to forgo this pleasure.

As soon as this was clear, Dr K rang up her best friend, and
best friend she proved to be. She postponed her appointments, found someone to look after the children, made sure
her husband had everything he needed and pre-cooked his
meals so as to be able to go with her friend.

The very thing Dr K had been trying to avoid for years was
now about to happen. When she joined the firm as the second
of two women surrounded by a host of men, she had soon
realized that she had to guard against projecting any kind of
erotic interest towards this particular man. She had to appear
as indifferent as possible, at best quite inconspicuous, so as to
be sure not to attract his eye. He treated the women in his
department with kind of cloying familiarity. Whenever he
was around, Dr K was overcome with a sense of yawning
boredom she found hard to suppress. But his position of
authority was unchallenged, and it was thus wise not to
attract attention. After all, nothing could be worse than to be
chosen by him and then not want to play ball. He was the type
to take revenge. Dr K loved her work and he was the channel
through which applications were either accepted or rejected
and new research projects either funded or allowed to run dry.
Anyway, her fears had now come true. It was not that he
looked at her any more meaningfully than before. There was
no indication, no tremor in his voice, no firm evidence of any
kind to suggest an imminent sexual assault; but she knew that
behind his intention to go with her, there lurked his further

intention to sleep with her and that this intention was
tantamount to an order. He was the same as ever but she had
always known that it would eventually come to this. In for a
penny, in for a pound. After all, it wasn't as if he were her first
employer. A successful woman has to be broken in. Dr K's
problem was not so much that she was surprised by this
unspoken proposition but that she had her scruples. She was
afraid of doing him an injustice. She hoped that her suspicions
were wrong. Yet she had no wish to put it to the test. After all,
she had had her share of experiences and had always been
able to rely on her instincts. Perhaps he is an exception, she
reasoned to herself, simply a nice man with no ulterior
motives. Her precautions and preconceptions might be totally
misplaced. For she was professional enough to have considered this possibility and her possible reactions before the
congress took place. What should she do if faced with it? It was
quite out of the question that she should be the one to take the
initiative.

Dr K was by no means a prude. She was quite capable of
turning a blind eye now and then. But one thing was certain
— she was no masochist and when she slept with someone
there had to be some kind of pleasure in it for her, however
slight. Even if it was her boss she was sleeping with. It did not
always have to be enjoyment of an erotic kind. It could equally
well be intellectual or some other kind of pleasure that, under
the circumstances, could only be achieved in bed. In short,
she had to feel she was doing it of her own free will. Dr K knew
that she was completely incapable of calculation in bed. So
she had already seriously sought a justification for getting into
bed with her director in order to save herself a lot of the
embarrassment that was bound to follow if she did not do so.
For however difficult it was to imply that he had any such
intentions at all, it was no less obvious to her that a rejection
was something he would never forgive. She would be made to

suffer the consequences of her behaviour. He was not one to let bygones be bygones.

His annoncement sent her into a state of panic. She stared at him in the canteen, asking herself which part of his body she could find attractive enough to enable her to go through with it. There just had to be something about him that she could find endearing, whether it be the way he moved, his mouth, his skin, the smell of his skin — but no, that of all things it could not be. He smelled sour. Was there anything to arouse enough erotic enthusiasm for her to forget the rest of him, unappetizing as it was, for as long as it would take? She thought about it objectively for a whole evening, but there was nothing she could find. To put it bluntly, she didn't feel like it at all.

Revolutionaries filed past in her mind's eye. People who sacrifice themselves for the sake of the cause. She felt so sorry for herself, she got drunk. But it was not the revolution that was at stake. She would not have the satisfaction of being rewarded for it afterwards by a grateful populace. On the contrary, it was something that had to happen in secret and be kept a secret. She wouldn't receive a medal for it. If all went well — and she would have to do well by him for this to be so — she would be able to continue doing her work. But if all went wrong, if she slipped up for as much as half a second, and he noticed she was play-acting, she would end up back at square one. She felt an uncontrollable surge of hatred towards her male colleagues who did not have to grapple with problems of this kind. They could look forward to the food when their director invited them out to a meal without first having to think about buying some disinfectant to mop up the vomit afterwards.

As it was, Dr K came to the conclusion that she was not the right person for this man. Even had she wanted to (and she would have loved to have wanted to), she couldn't — which is why she asked her girlfriend to come too. Her job was to be right there next to Dr K all the time, bright and cheerful. She wasn't to stir from her side or leave her alone with the director for a single second. At the same time, she was to display such charm and show such naivety that the director would not, under any circumstances, be able to interpret her being there as an insult. He must not suspect the plan. They must not put a foot wrong.

Her friend did her job brilliantly. She beamed away next to Dr K while the latter declared for the umpteenth time what an extraordinarily nice director they had as head of the department in which she had had the good fortune to work for so long now. She never tired of stressing that she enjoyed his special tutelage. A director, moreover, who made a point of supporting women. Only the best, he added gallantly.

Unfortunately, it had been too late for her friend to find a hotel room and she had to share Dr K's double bed. To make doubly sure, Dr K had also mentioned having a headache and the first signs of 'flu. Her friend had casually mentioned that Dr K snored which she, for her part, thought was going too far. After the ceremony, the three of them sat opposite one another in the hotel bar, fixed grins on their faces. The director was all smiles and went on smiling even after his nostrils started flaring in anger. Was it anger or was he just tired too, Dr K wondered when she was finally in her room alone with her friend and, exhausted, they both had a glass of cognac.

— Was I right to ask you?

— Am I worth the money, then? her friend wanted to know in reply. After all, her being there had its price.

Yes, she also thought that Dr K had been right but there was no way it could be proved conclusively. He was not one of those cocksure breast-grabbers with whom you at least know where you are. Nor was it a question of sexuality even. After all, he could buy himself a young woman if that was what he was after. It was Dr K's self-assurance that made her so attractive. It took a real man to crack that.

A year passed and nothing happened. He forwarded her applications, he supported her, he advised her. She was his prize exhibit. She was already on the verge of inwardly asking his forgiveness. Perhaps his going there with her really had been meant quite unselfishly and kindly. What stopped her from actually apologizing was the uneasy thought that he could be a sadist. Perhaps he wanted to keep her in suspense so as to savour her subsequent defeat all the more? There was also the possibility that he was not even aware of his thirst for revenge. She carried on working as usual but she was waiting for the moment when he would let the cat out of the bag.

One day he informed her kindly, albeit without a convincing reason, that he would not be forwarding her proposal. It was a waste of money to go on subsidizing the project any longer. It had no future. The whole approach was wrong, a dead-end. She defended herself, of course, and insisted that he specify the reasons. But he was in a position not to have to give reasons. He didn't want to and that was that. Besides, it was true that her approach was unconventional and furthermore it was properly qualified assistants that she really needed. In theory she had been prepared for this blow for a long time but it still hurt when it came. She had to begin again from scratch. She wondered what it was that made her go on being polite and why on earth she had to start crying on top of everything else. It was embarrassing for him. He fetched her a fresh cup of coffee and a schnaps. He handed her a handkerchief. Dr K cordially shook hands with this rotten little arsehole, this wanker, who had even had the gall to keep her up to date on his digestive problems and tell her all about his next holiday plans before rejecting her proposal.

She went to the Ladies, washed her face, powdered her nose and made herself up. She couldn't afford to look all puffy.

THE BIRTHDAY GUEST

The party was over. Only two guests remained, Guest A and Guest B. Ms K had flirted a little with Guest A. She wanted to ask him to stay the night. But he left her, suspecting she had something going with Guest B. That was not so. But it was obvious to Ms K that Guest B wanted to stay the night.

Ms K was furious at the way Guest B just stayed on as if it were the most natural thing in the world. But more than anything else, she was tired. And, besides, deep down in her heart she didn't even care whether A or B stayed or left. She had other worries. She certainly didn't feel like explaining anything. That was her main concern. Guest B thought Ms K was in need of love. There was a slight suggestion of the social worker in his manner as he climbed into her bed without so much as a by-your-leave. Ms K looked on in amazement and resigned herself to the inevitable. Guest B was convinced that he was now about to treat Ms K to something extra special. Ms K said nothing. She didn't feel like discussing things. Nor did she want to throw him out. He wouldn't have understood that and, what was more important, she would have had to explain even more then. So she lay down next to him, it was her bed. To simplify matters, she had already stripped completely. She meant to avoid talking because she knew he was a dogmatist, though forever espousing a different cause. At the moment his main concern was to be 'gentle' and 'understanding', he was fired with enthusiasm for doing things 'together'. She kissed him to stop him talking. She hugged him. And, as she did so, she realized that she didn't have the slightest desire to sleep with this man who preached 'desire' as part of his political platform. It was the last thing she wanted to do and she told him so. I don't want to, she said kindly. Even that he could understand, after all he considered her repressed. He had just completed a course on breathing and treated the uninitiated with blind arrogance. Just as he used to when he still distributed leaflets at six o'clock in the morning outside the factory gates. But she didn't care what he thought, just as long as he left her in peace. He had no idea how arrogant she was. He had once stared in amazement at a slip of paper with the words 'My heart belongs to my head'. It was a quote she had copied out and he had secretly smiled to himself knowingly.

Before going to sleep, he informed her that he wanted to have a nice and relaxed breakfast with her the next day, and then they could tidy up together — how she hated that word. It had been a big party and tidying up would take hours. In fact, he was the first man she knew who had offered to do this. It could be so nice, having the help, but she knew that she would prefer to slave away all day on her own rather then endure his gentle embrace any longer.

He really was trying to be helpful, while Ms K gritted her teeth and kept a tight control on herself. She felt she was being harsh and unfair. But suddenly she insisted it was enough just to clear the plates and glasses out into the kitchen and to put the rubbish in the bin. As far as she was concerned, he could throw away the plates and glasses too, while he was about it. There was absolutely no need to start spring cleaning, she declared on the verge of hysterics, although this was a blatant lie. To get rid of him, she suggested they go for a walk. They walked along side by side in silence. She was fed up and set a quick pace, he was cheerful — it went with his new image. Not only that, he also seemed to have set his mind on helping her to relax. He really tried hard and he meant no harm. He wished for her sake that she could also learn to breathe properly and share an experience that had once been foreign to him too. When they arrived back at her door he really wanted to go up and have a cup of tea with her, but she swiftly kissed him goodbye and, with a sense of immediate relief, went to bed on her own.

THE FAITH HEALER

Ms K had suffered from a severe cold twice a year for as long as she could remember. None of the medicines, whether conventional or homeopathic, were any help at any time during her illness. She simply had to grin and bear it and, for a long time, it was the only thing of regularity in her life: seven days twice a year, two of them in bed.

Of all days, the man she was on the point of falling in love with just had to visit her on the worst. Within an hour she had already used up eight packs of the ten-a-pack tissues. There was no way her nose would stop running and it was painfully sore. Her throat was swollen, her head ached and she was sweating and shivering in turns. She could have died of embarrassment, she looked so awful. There she lay among the cushions hardly able to raise a smile and allowed him to bring her a hot lemon drink. Perhaps, she thought, it's just as well it's happening this way, perhaps he'll be so put off he won't show up again. After all, men normally respond to appearances. It would save them the host of problems that she vaguely anticipated. But, to her astonishment, he lay down next to her and stayed. She protested with the little that remained of her sense of reason and conventionality to protect him from infection. He nudged up against her. She could feel his body along her back and she said no more. She was overwhelmed by the feeling that nothing more could happen to her now, she was at home, she was a baby again. They turned towards each other. Their skin joined from head to toe. Pore to pore. Hair to hair. It intertwined. It would tear open terrible wounds to separate them again. They clung to each other as a virus clings to the cell wall of another virus. His arms and legs were an extension of hers. She could no longer tell the difference. The nerves of one pierced the skin of the other. And as he entered her, her nose stopped running, her sore throat gradually vanished, her head cleared and her temperature dropped. Half an hour later she had fully recovered. And she knew she was now immune. She would never catch a cold again as long as she could lay her skin to his. She thought only death would part them, but she was wrong.

When he ran off, and she didn't know why, she felt dismembered for years. It was a serious condition that affected over fifty percent of her body. It was a miracle she survived, even if it was with the most dreadful disfiguring scars, invisible to the naked eye. Night after night she screamed in agony, her skin was so painful. But she remained immune to colds. 'Flu epidemics raged all around her, one virus after another. Other people would take precautions, have their inoculations, and steer clear of anyone who might be infected, but she could sit down among them and drink from the same cup. She knew she wouldn't catch anything. It wasn't until ten years later that she woke up one morning with a cold.

TALKING AMONG THEMSELVES

Why are we telling each other all this? Why can't we stop talking about them?
— What else do you want us to do?
— Something new.
— Without them?
— I don't know.
The three Ms K were standing next to one another looking out of the window. It was lunchtime. A young man was trudging past in a pullover he'd knitted himself. He looked up into the three earnest pairs of eyes that were fixed on him, looked away quickly and made off at the double.
— He's scared. Isn't it sickening?

They were all three depressed. 'Is this what you thought it would be like to be self-confident?' The question hung in the warm air of the room for a long time.

They stood there following the man with their eyes until he had become a tiny speck and finally disappeared behind a pile of white snow. Later on, as they were still staring out of the window, a couple came down the street.
— She's a librarian, he's a professor, said Ms K.

She had put her arm through his and was leaning against him heavily at an awkward angle while he was attempting to hold himself particularly upright. She was chattering away at him brightly. Too brightly.

A ridiculous sight. They knew the woman. They had been sitting at neighbouring tables on their first night together at the inn. The three Ms K at one table and this couple, along with another couple and a single lady, at the other. In the middle of their lively, five-way conversation, the woman out there had suddenly thrown her arms around her already rather stout and greying boyfriend, showering him with childish endearments and drawing the attention of her table companions, especially the single lady, to her happiness in the way dog or child owners often do when they require those present to give their immediate and undivided attention to some particularly successful display of good manners on the part of their child or to a trick performed by their dachshund. This spontaneous demonstrative eruption instantly stunned both tables into a state of numb bewilderment and it took quite a while for the people at the next table to find a way of resuming their conversation without appearing impolite.

— If he runs off one day and leaves her. . .

— He won't run off. He'll just have a bit on the side. Don't you kid yourself, she's one of those that are most in demand.

Baffled, they went on staring out of the window, into the whiteness.

— What's so wrong with us?

— The official facts hardly ever fit in with my own personal experience, the pregnant woman said hesitantly. I always hope I'm wrong. Either they are wrong or I am wrong. So it's reality I have a problem with.

— Perhaps we should give up the idea that liberation brings happiness.

— But even the squatters hold on to a house sometimes. And the Sandinistas have had their victories. . .

They watched the old lush enviously as he waddled by outside with his woman on his arm. The couple had already receded into the distance yet their two thin lines were still just visible — one upright and the other leaning.

— Not all men are fools, the pregnant one said, looking around in a self-confident sort of way.

There was no response. The elder one had turned away from the window; she poured some cognac into a glass and absentmindedly leafed through a pile of magazines.

— *Don't forget, she said after a while, that here we are talking about the very cream of men in arts and politics and science. None of your common-or-garden types who've just popped up from nowhere. They are our lovers.*

As she said this, she flicked the photo of a man they all knew. Then they all leant over the magazines, poring over the pictures. They tried guessing the ages of the politicians and always got it wrong. They could not work out the system by which the people in the photographs aged. The more successful they were, the more their features appeared to evaporate.

— *It's the stress that does it, Ms K said.*

Then they read the television guide and discovered that that evening ten different men, most of whom they knew, would be discussing the ways in which art and politics influence one another.

— *They will have their discussion and think no further of it. Those friends of ours.*

— *Why are we so desperate for them to be our friends? Why do we have to insist on that, on top of everything else? Why can't we just leave them?*

— *We're afraid of admitting we've lost.*

— *Now we're paying the price, said the one in the middle, for not having fitted in well enough, for having had too much of a good time or whatever you want to call it.*

— *Fulfilled ourselves, said the older one.*

— *If we had been more afraid, we'd have been less inquisitive, know less as a result and Fleshpots out there on his walk would be able to impress us with his experience of life. Indeed, we'd even be grateful to him for deigning to notice us and we'd not feel lonely any more.*

Ms K read the village's 'programme of events' and saw that the weekly film was showing that evening. They decided to go, because it was a Belmondo film and at least he has good muscles.

THE TELEPHONE CALL

For a few months Ms K lived happily together with a man. But it was not long before complications from previous relationships twisted up inside him forming such knots of anxiety and doubt that he sought release in bouts of aggression, minor at first but then more and more violent, hitting out blindly in all directions. After she'd been knocked senseless by him several times and finally ended up with a fractured skull, it was all over between them. She hoped that once he had regained his sanity he would realize how violent he had been and apologize to her. The possibility of this ever happening had long since entered the realm of the miraculous when, years later, the telephone rang, waking Ms K in the middle of the night. Ms K groped for the receiver, still groggy from the tablets she had been taking fairly regularly since he had moved out. A man at the other end, this very man, was saying his name. — Who? she heard herself ask although her body, which had responded by breaking out in a sweat, already knew who it was. Her befuddled brain heard him repeat both forename and surname. Considering the nature of their acquaintance, the formality of this slowly seeped into her clouded mind as something strangely amusing. She looked at the clock for further proof that this was really happening. It was twenty to five on a winter's morning.

— He had behaved badly, said the voice, and he was sorry. Could he be so bold as to come and see her?

— Yes, she said, he should be so bold. Her head was hanging uncomfortably over the edge of the bed and the weight of her body was pressing her wrist against the wood as she held the receiver.

— Go on, say something, he said.

What on earth should she say?

— Yes, she said, he should just come, she said. Yes, just come, she repeated in a tight voice for the fifth time by now.

— Yes, he said hesitantly, he would, and hung up.

Excited and delighted, she told her best friend about the early morning telephone call, clothing the remaining traces of irritation at his repeatedly telling her to 'go on and say something' in misgivings that she might still have been rather grumpy from the tablets and not polite enough.

— Why doesn't he ring up in the daytime? her friend asked sensibly. — Why does he have to take you by surprise in the middle of the night, after all this time? Does he want you to forgive him for nothing first? Remorse without risk? Don't start getting sentimental, now.

Three days after the telephone call, Ms K was consumed by nervousness and doubt. After two weeks she gave up all hope and stopped waiting for him to come. She secretly went through her memory, testing each item to see if it could be used in evidence. The mark made by the edge of the bed cutting into her wrist had long since disappeared and it didn't prove anything anyway.

Four weeks later her friend cautiously enquired whether Ms K was quite sure that there really had been a telephone call.

After all, if you want something really badly, she said, it was all too easy to dream it had come true.

— Perhaps it was just you hoping so much that he would apologize, she suggested, offering her friend an easy way out with her kind, observant scepticism.

The incident wasn't mentioned again. Years later, Ms K heard the story the man had been telling of his serious efforts to make up with her, from other friends of hers. They knew all about how determined she had been to hate the man and how impervious she had been to the man's apologies while he, despite the best of intentions, had resigned himself to give up after trying to arrange a meeting by telephone.

— At least my senses didn't delude me, thought Ms K with relief. She had become altogether less demanding by now.

TALKING AMONG THEMSELVES

I always wanted a son, Ms K said after a while.
— *Me too, said the other.*
— *And what if it had been a daughter?*
— *She'd probably be a perfect little monster.*
— *Why didn't you want a daughter?*
— *Put it down to my arrogance, if you like. And my own unhappiness. I wanted the greatest prize. I envy you being able to want a daughter.*
— *So there is progress, after all, Ms K ventured, grinning contentedly.*
— *Or it may be cowardice, for all I know.*
— *One look at me and my father never collected the gold bracelet he had already ordered from the jeweller's. My mother felt guilty. She wasn't even capable of producing a son. Too stupid even for that, my father used to say.*
— *And you thought you were better than your mother? Ms K stared at her in amazement.*
— *There's the story about the making of a hero. Do you want to hear it?*

THE MAKING OF A HERO

The hero-to-be of countless dreams and disappointments, the man who had given more than one woman the feeling of being understood for the first time in her life — for he was so adoring and fairly melted into their caressing hands — was born to an SS officer and his wife in August 1943. He was their third child and first son. It is known that the father would not allow his wife to sleep with her hands under the blanket, for propriety's sake. The mother told her children this much later, after the divorce. By then she was able to say with a laugh:

— He simply wouldn't allow me to sleep with my hands under the blanket.

With that she had the children on her side. They were glad to be rid of him. He was still alive somewhere, but completely cut off from his offspring. How can a woman share a bed with a husband who won't allow her to put her hands under the blanket? her son asked in a voice that she dreaded.

— What did he threaten to do then? he wanted to know later.

The mother was reluctant to answer that. The question alone was enough to upset her. He just didn't understand things like that, she said evasively. Had he threatened her or had she just learnt to be afraid of men, to keep her eyes to herself? Her being so obedient disconcerted the man although he thought it was natural, took it for granted, and would have been very surprised had she not been. But though he didn't realize it, it made him aggressive. After all, it was part of his job to order people about. One harsh word from him and his wife cringed like a dog, just like the people he had to load up during the day. And yet at first, this tone of voice towards his wife had just slipped out by mistake when something didn't suit him. It was quite unintentional. He just couldn't adjust so quickly.

Later, he tried it out systematically. It was his way of expressing his disbelief. He would use the same gestures, the same voice at home as he did out of the house. He wanted to know how far he could go. He could go as far as he liked. It was not something he was consciously aware of, just a feeling that hardened inside him. The mother feared these experiments. He only had to look in a particular way and she gave in to him. She always obeyed in advance. She never defended herself. She would weep, but swallowed it all. He was a little wimp who had been blown up into giant proportions in her mind. He would never have harmed her. He would have felt something at last. She found refuge in total weakness.

He went to work every morning to do his duty. Something connected with the railways. His wife didn't know exactly what. Whatever it was it had to do with reallocating the consignments that arrived by train from all points of the compass. Sometimes he would even have to ride along on one of the trains, and then he would return home in the evening, tightlipped, from some wretched place in the middle of nowhere: Berum, Dalum, Esterwegen, Bergen, Moorhausen, Sandbostel or whatever their names were. There weren't many men who weren't sent to the front because they had essential war work to do at home. It was so essential it was classified under the security regulations. Not even his wife was allowed to ask any questions. She was a good wife if she willingly bit her lips, that way she was playing her part on the home front, as it were. However, her husband did go so far as to hint that his work was no piece of cake and that personal sacrifices had to be made for the sake of the cause.

'You can't make an omelet without breaking eggs' was one of the stock sayings he used to shrug off things he didn't himself understand. You can't always have everything your own way. He had to grit his teeth often enough too. As his wife, she was treated with formal regard when she went shopping. The very name SS spread a chill. She found the whole thing rather disturbing. Her husband's work was men's business, rather like sexuality. Just as it was only proper for women to enter marriage as virgins, it was obviously equally taken for granted that their husbands would be experienced in bed without anyone ever talking about where that experience came from. They were the teachers as far as that was concerned too, just like in everything else. He left the house purposefully and entered it purposefully. But none of it was ever discussed. Of course, she was used to holding her tongue from an early age, as were all girls who wanted to pass as well-bred.

One night in August he had come home silent and morose, muttered something about the last place on earth and work fit for dogs, closed the flowery curtains, hung his uniform over the chair, lay down next to her and finally reached out to grab her. Then he kissed her. She turned her face so he couldn't touch her mouth, but in a way that wouldn't offend him. The man had a right of access to her. It never entered her head that it could be different, that there could be relaxed moments in life, free from domination and hierarchy, free from the immediate call of duty. It had been drummed into her at an early age that giving birth to her children would be a painful business. She stood by this knowledge and was not at all surprised when it turned out the way that everyone had said it would. All she realized after her marriage was that the 'painful business' referred to the whole thing. Intercourse included. She put her arms round her husband. He liked it that way, and besides it was part of her duty. That was what it meant to be married.

The man silently and disenchantedly fucked his wife and fucked a new German family into existence. He was limping along behind the times, as it were, and dimly aware of it too. Stalingrad had fallen, the Wehrmacht had surrendered in Africa, the Allies had landed on Sicily, in Italy the Fascist Party had been disbanded and the Uprising was raging in the Warsaw ghetto. But here, in this bed, he was fathering a family. It was to have at least one son in it for then, and only then, would it be a proper family. The man was confused. It was impossible to reconcile his duties with the dreams he had of his duties. He would drive out of his head the very images he would have to return to in the morning. For a few seconds he sensed the possibility of letting go, being a prisoner, changing places, becoming an object, being without obligations towards the Great and Good. More than anything else he wished he did not have beneath him this stuffed owl of a wife, whom he was now ramming with positive hatred. He suppressed a groan. The last come, when it spilled out of him, was warm yet quick to grow cold and slimy. It was left untouched, then immediately and discreetly wiped away with her nightdress.

She gritted her teeth. Life was hard, but praise be to He who made things hard. At least she had the consolation that the sacrifice she was making now — and she only called it such to herself in secret — would be exchanged for social recognition after the birth of a child. Motherhood had made her important for the first time in her life. She passed for the German mother on the posters when she went out holding her children by the hand. People jumped up for her in the tram. That gave her some sense of bearing. The importance she had gained through motherhood would also be expressed in the official birth announcement: '... has presented the Fatherland with a son.' She, at one with the Great Good. It gave a sense of fulfilment, despite everything. It surrounded her person with the aura of national importance. That was new, although she was happiest of all when she had her period because he did not sleep with her then. At intervals, she would suppress the unsavoury feeling she had of being nothing more than some kind of transitional processing plant or a transit camp for human material, that was more like it. An internment camp for embryos. Each child was given just one name. The children mustn't be spoilt. It would be the worst imaginable crime she could commit as a mother. That was what she had been taught and she thought no more of it. The children needed toughening up. And toughened up they were. Thank God they were still too small to be called up and duty to the Fatherland had its limits. That is what she secretly thought sometimes. The son had not even been born yet. And being a mother, she herself would not be liable for the compulsory national service that might be introduced. There had been so many rumours about it recently. Lying one on top of the other like this, husband and wife each carried on their own silent soliloquy. Had a man been listening, he would have wept for pity. Had a woman been listening, she would have wept for pity.

That night in August egg and sperm united. The dull silence embedded itself in the cell walls as did the news that had been heard, though not discussed — the activities of dissident students in Munich, the collapse of the Eastern Front, Iran's declaration of war, the bombing raids on German cities — it was all there, absorbed, encapsulated and unresolved. Their son received the first shock of his life in an embryonic state. While still in the womb he had stretched out towards his mother's hands in search of comfort. But her hands rarely rested on her belly and they were snatched away immediately as soon as the man's voice, his father's voice, was heard. The father did not permit her to caress the children. Caressing makes them soft. What kind of work is it that is so hard it can't be done by a soft-hearted man? However, the son in question had still not arrived. He was a mere supposition. He was only just beginning to be entertained as a possibility when the man came home one evening in September happier than he had been for a long time. There was a victory to be chalked up. The sudden panic that overcame him on occasion when struck by the awful possibility that it might all end differently than he imagined, that all his sacrifices might have been in vain, the panic that blocked his brain and robbed him of all imagination was gone for one night at least. In the best of moods, the man slept with his wife. He called her 'my little mouse' and nibbled her ear. Mussolini had been rescued from imprisonment in Gran Sasso. And there was the Republic of Salo even if the cowardly Italians were flocking to join the Yugoslav partisans. But today he did not yell. He was elated, the woman relaxed. She told him of her sweet suspicion.

This was the time the Hungarian Jews were being deported to Auschwitz. Drastic organizational problems deep into the Reich. How much filtered through to the mother and what effect did it have on intercourse and the tremors that rocked the son? This was the time when she reflected that some day she would no longer want this man at her side. She listened closely when she heard talk of divorce and began to consider it as a possibility for herself. However, she was to become pregnant again several times before it came to that.

She had imagined love to be less cruel. Later, she burst into tears and had migraines when her child wanted to know why she had stayed with this brute for so long. The mother feigned weakness. She exaggerated his brutality. She hadn't had a chance against this little man in the photos. The son cut his father out of the photos. It was irritating that he actually

looked rather pleasant. He didn't want it always there before
his eyes.

It had been instilled into the child that if he loved his
mother he should refrain from asking any questions that
could cause her unhappiness. Should he still insist, then he
was to blame for his mother's tears. Love, the boy learnt,
means suppressing your own feelings. Love means making
sacrifices. If he liked something she didn't like he has to lie to
her and spare her feelings. For she is terrified of the truth.
Silently, through her tears, she implores him to deceive her.
And he learns the lesson perfectly.

The boy develops a yearning for abundance and warmth.
At times, when lying in the embrace of a woman, her hands
touching him, his father's voice dimly echoes in his memory.
He becomes confused then, when her hands stay there,
touching him. He feels something is wrong. His dear good
mother used to snatch her hands away. He can't trust these
hands. If he trusts these hands, he doesn't trust his mother. He
pushes the hands away. And looks for them again. He begins
to deceive his mother, so as not to disillusion her, and yet
wanting to keep for himself the warmth of these other hands.
He had to deceive her, otherwise he would be just as cruel as
his father. He would be causing her pain. His father, however,
is the socially tolerated monster. The whole of society sides
with his mother. After all, she divorced the man and purified
herself. Good must be distinguished from bad and the two
must be kept nicely separate. The son is on the good side. He
spares his mother's feelings. He doesn't make her cry. And
when his doubts torment him, he drinks. It all comes out
when he is drunk, but it doesn't count then. Still a youth he
stows away to America on a freighter. He writes postcards in
advance and arranges for a friend to send them to his mother
once a week from southern Germany. The cards describe his
cycle tours and nights at the YMCA. His mother is glad her

son has turned out so well. His hands are on top of the blanket. There is no end to the number of woollen socks she knits for his feet. Warm socks for his feet, for the hands on top of the blanket. That's the way he will learn to be a good man. But his skin longs for warmth and comes out in spots.

He cannot imagine displaying his true feelings without losing affection in return. The price for his warm feet is silence. He longs to be loved. Silence is part of it. It was a part of his making that had somehow remained with him.

EXPEDITION WITH A UFO

Ms K met Heinz S on the library steps. She was on her way out, he was on his way in. They hadn't seen each other for almost fifteen years. His hair had turned grey now and he had two different academic degrees but he still had the same easily frightened grey eyes with long eyelashes and the same even way of walking. They were both delighted. They chatted for a while on the steps, then he escorted her to a private view at which she drank cheap wine and got drunk. He took her home in his car, stopping at every second tree so that she only had to open the door and lean out to be sick. He even put her to bed. He rang her up the next day and they made a dinner date to catch up on the past fifteen years during which they had had nothing to do with each other. In fact, it was the first time in their lives that they had ever really talked to each other properly, as they had previously only ever had distant contact with one another through friends of friends and by studying the same courses, breathing the same air, having similar lifestyles, asking similar questions. So they didn't really know each other at all, yet they had seen each other regularly and seeing each other so often had bred a certain affinity between them. The fact that they were now talking on the telephone was a phenomenon comparable to the sort of thing a Bavarian might feel chancing upon another Bavarian in the middle of Australia. Surrounded by so much that is foreign, there is suddenly something they have in common.

While they were talking on the telephone, Heinz S asked Ms K whether she had a balcony. Ms K said no. When he then arrived to pick her up for their date he was carrying a beautiful oleander tree in a pot so huge he could hardly get his hands round it. Oleander is an outdoor shrub that will die if kept indoors. A week later, almost all the leaves had fallen off or turned yellow whereupon Ms K left the window open. This suited the plant, which recovered, but not her. A gift with a snag, she mused, thinking of winter.

They spent a lively evening at an expensive restaurant and, after exchanging ideas on life in general and talking about their plans for the future, their career prospects and politics, Heinz S launched into a vivid description of the mountains and the joys of mountain walking only to conclude despondently that his girlfriend wasn't particularly fond of the mountains and so it was a pleasure he hardly ever came by nowadays. Ms K had enjoyed listening to him. She could just see the high Alpine meadows, the cows, the peace and quiet, the flowers before her very eyes. She suggested he take her along for a few days on one of his hikes. Heinz S was delighted with the idea but suddenly Ms K saw delight give way to anxiety. He changed the subject abruptly. But Ms K took it up again, she simply could not miss the sight of him chewing over the idea further. In the end, he came out with it. He had to discuss the situation with his girlfriend first. She was his life, he said rather pathetically, and under no circumstances did he wish to jeopardize their relationship. Being slightly sentimental herself, Ms K was quite captivated by this objection. She rather envied his girlfriend although she knew that, in her shoes, she wouldn't have been able to bear the anxiety in his words. She remembered the remark that had been thrown at her in a similar situation: I'm not like soap, you know, I don't get used up.

As things turned out, his girlfriend gave her consent. Heinz S visited Ms K twice more to discuss their 'basic' understanding of the trip. He had a long list of problems he wished to resolve before they left. What would they do if they could no longer stand the sight of each other after two days? What happened if one of them wanted to walk in one direction and the other in another direction? Ms K felt unable to say anything 'basic' to all this. They would just separate if things unexpectedly went wrong, she said deliberately. Heinz S spread out his maps in front of Ms K. He worked out a number of possible routes and had her give them her blessing. Not knowing the mountains, she agreed to everything he proposed. She willingly placed herself in his hands.

They agreed not to overdo things to start with, to make allowances for Ms K's inexperience, to limit the hike to a week and to find a compromise between his love of glaciers and scree slopes and her love of cows and mountain pastures. Ms K was amazed at the assortment of maps he had: maps showing where the huts were, guide books stating when the huts were staffed, weather maps. He appeared to be unsure of himself as he pieced together the route. And she eventually realized that he was afraid of her and she did her best to make him understand that she wouldn't hold it against him if anything went wrong. Feeling unexpectedly irritated, she said they should just wait and see what happened. The easy atmosphere had suddenly disappeared, and Ms K knew from experience that this mixture of admiration and anxiety would only lead to aggression and, again, she would be the one to end up suffering for it. For a moment she remembered the man with whom travelling had been such a marvellously easy and enjoyable affair. But he was gone now, travelling with some other woman.

The expedition began at Munich airport with Heinz S picking up Ms K in his new car. They greeted each other with an awkward hug and, sitting self-consciously next to each other, they proceeded to drive up into the mountains. He countered Ms K's front seat hysteria with repeated assurances that he was an excellent driver, a statement that has absolutely no effect on hysterical front seat passengers. They arrived in South Tyrol and after supper, during which he twice bent down under the table to take a pill, they drove on to the site they had previously chosen for the night. They intended to sleep in the car. It was equipped with all the necessaries, food, water, a stove, tools and mattresses. But neither of them could sleep. The close quarters, the noise of the lorries on the road and the chirping of the crickets put them both on edge. Ms K swallowed a sedative she had packed just in case.

At seven o'clock the next morning — they intended to set off early into the mountains — they discovered that they had parked at a crossing of dirt tracks right next to a rubbish dump. Heinz S set up the camping gaz and a saucepan and explained to a dumbfounded Ms K that he intended to 'boil up', as the scouts used to say. Ms K couldn't help collapsing into a fit of laughter, seeing as they were in sight of an espresso bar a hundred yards away which would serve them breakfast. Rather hesitantly, Heinz S ended up laughing too. They then proceeded to pack their rucksacks in true mountaineering fashion. She had followed all his instructions and was able to prove to his satisfaction that nothing vital was missing. She only haggled over the sleeping bag, but lost out there, and over the quantity of food to take with them. She insisted that the muesli bars would do for her and categorically rejected his offer to carry food for her, too. He had bought provisions to last over a week: several kilos of sausages, bread and tinned food all of which he stowed away in his rucksack. In the end, his weighed twenty kilos, hers half that, which she still found heavy enough.

They had agreed beforehand that Heinz S would part company with her for a one-day excursion into the High Alps if they should meet up with people in one of the huts who

wanted to climb up higher, for which Ms K possessed neither
the expertise, the equipment nor the physical fitness. He had
bought crampons in Munich just the previous day for this
purpose. However, it now transpired that they didn't fit so he
asked Ms K to allow him to make a small detour into the
nearest village to buy some new ones. It was his last chance
since they would not be coming down into the valley for the
next seven days. He apologized several times for upsetting the
timetable they had worked out and it was all his fault. But
there were no crampons to be found in the first village they
came to. Nor in the second. By that time it was midday and the
shops had closed. They would not open again until four
o'clock in the afternoon. The most sensible thing seemed to be
to drive into the nearest town of any size, Merano, in the hope
that it would be different there. It wasn't. It was one o'clock
and they had three hours to wait until the shops opened again
and — hopefully — they could find the right size crampons.
Heinz S was frightfully embarrassed about the whole business
for the day he had so meticulously planned and with it their
entire programme was now slipping away. Ms K didn't mind
about this at all. On the contrary, she was positively delighted.
Besides, the town was new to her. All the same, she was glad
she hadn't been the one to forget something vital. And she
would have been happier still if he hadn't apologized so often.
She wasn't cross with him at all but he refused to believe it.
During the afternoon a situation developed such as Ms K had
had often enough with a girlfriend of hers and simply hated.
This friend would go on and on apologizing for some silly but
rather irrelevant thing she had done until Ms K realized that
all she wanted was for her to repeat her protestations over and
over. If she didn't protest, it was a sure sign that Ms K had not
been telling the truth and must still be cross. Ms K refused to
go along with this kind of game and stopped after having
repeated her protestations three times at the most. This

regularly resulted in her friend showering her with abuse. Things were never far off ending like Chekhov's short story in which a man inadvertently sneezes down another man's neck in the theatre and apologizes for it so often and at such length that the other loses his patience with this fellow who can't grasp that his apology has been accepted and beats him to death. Ms K told this story with a laugh as a warning.

By late afternoon their purchases had been made. They parked the car in the little village they had chosen high up in the mountains and, changing their original plan, decided to walk only as far as the next hut and spend the night there. It was warm, but not too warm, just right to get into the swing of things. They had only been walking uphill for twenty minutes when Heinz S noticed that he was getting blisters on his feet. Before they had left Cologne he had warned her about the horrors of having blisters on your feet. Beginners who were unused to walking in the mountains were particularly liable to get them as they were careless about wearing the right kind of socks and shoes. Ms K had at once taken his warnings seriously and made the appropriate purchases and preparations. Heinz S was wearing the heaviest of the three pairs of mountaineering boots he had packed into the car, just in case. They were for walking above the snow line and weighed nearly a kilo each. Now instead of immediately sticking a plaster, of which Ms K had a plentiful supply, over the sore spot, he gritted his teeth and plodded on. He probably wanted to avoid causing yet another delay in their itinerary so soon after the last. Earlier, Heinz S had been explaining to Ms K that it was stretching oneself to the limits that made hikes of this kind so stimulating. It seemed to her that he had almost reached his by now. Ms K was intrigued by this. But, after all, she could hardly oblige him to accept the plaster, let alone force him to turn back. With his feet hurting, his overladen rucksack on his back, the plastic bag containing his new

crampons in one hand and the map in the other, he staggered
on in front of Ms K along wide and well-marked footpaths —
it was like going for a walk in a park, thought Ms K —
cautioning her every now and then not to stop because she
would suffer for it if she did, it was not good mountaineering
practice. But she stopped all the same, behind his back, to
recover from the mild spells of dizziness she was experiencing
and to take in the view which was, after all, what she had come
for. Ms K was afraid she had bitten off more than she could
chew. Then there was the hut at last. The sun was setting.
Tyroleans were there with their green aprons and guttural
speech. It was like being in *Heidi*. Schnaps was served
followed by a good wine. They had bread dumplings to eat
and then, during dessert, Heinz S again half disappeared
under the table to take his little pill. What was he on, Ms K
wondered. But he shook his head. He would tell her some
other time, maybe. It must be something catching, Ms K
thought. She was content. They were so exhausted they didn't
talk much. He apologized for being so disorganized and
spoiling their first day. It wasn't spoilt, said Ms K. She
wouldn't have been able to go any further anyway.

It was quiet up here. It smelt good. Every now and then, a
distant sound echoed up from the valley. They were given a
room with bunk beds.

Forestry workers could get up this far by tractor. The next
morning, some of them were driving back down to the village
where they had parked their car. Ms K's rucksack was too
heavy for her, so bit by bit she gathered together the things
she didn't need — it amounted to half a kilo in the end — and
asked them to take them down to the village with them. Heinz
S could not be persuaded to do without at least two kilos of
food. He conjured up dreadful visions of sudden breaks in the
weather, being cut off, heavy mist, thunderstorms and hail,
and on each occasion they would have to stick it out wherever

they were, for days at a time maybe. Ms K was quite willing to believe him and it all seemed very sensible for higher up in the mountains, but every time she risked a glance down into the valley that fine morning she could see little cars driving along a stretch of road. They did not yet appear to be that far removed from civilization. But she didn't say anything; after all, he was the experienced one.

The schedule for the second day's walk involved climbing over a ridge into the next valley. Now and then people would overtake the two hikers, passing nimbly by without packs, some in trainers, and greet them with a 'Good day', to which Ms K responded with a 'Hallo'. She was concentrating on the piece of ground and the stones at her feet. If she gave up now, turning back would be just as gruelling as the path that still lay before them. So she went on. Ms K wondered how much willpower Heinz S was having to muster as he swayed frequently under the weight of his rucksack for, that day too, he was still carrying the plastic bag containing his crampons as there was no room to attach them to his rucksack. Not only was there a blister on his foot that morning, but it was severely inflamed and must have been extremely painful. He rejected Ms K's suggestion that they wait until his foot was all right again before going on any further. He was behaving like an escaped prisoner from a Siberian labour camp, she thought, stepping back from nothing, no matter how painful or exhausting, to save his skin. It was then that the term UFO first occurred to her and after that it was the word she secretly used to describe him behind his back. She simply could not make him out.

The numbers of the paths marked on their maps had been painted on rocks. However, when they followed the directions indicated, they found the paths would end or have quite different numbers. Ms K learnt that Italian maps were no good at all. They just weren't accurate. They had been following paths that weren't shown on the map, and there were other paths, clearly numbered on the map, that had been numbered quite differently in reality etc. He was constantly grumbling about these discrepancies, however significant or insignificant they might be, but then again he would jump for joy to discover that the right-hand bend before them was actually marked on the map. He stopped at least every five hundred yards to compare. Every now and then they would meet other people. If there was a man among them he was bound to be holding a map in his hand and the two of them, true hikers that they were, would compare notes and curse at what they came up with. Yesterday, they had even sat huddled together in the mountain hut poring over their maps, Ms K had noticed that at once. And the women sat there too, leaning towards the men as courtesy and cleverness required. Occasionally they would murmur 'hm, hm', eyes empty, but if their eyes chanced to meet they would guiltily turn their heads and look away before an irresistible grin settled on their faces, and focus again on their husbands who were busy puzzling out the next stages of the route.

Their next objective was a lake surrounded by scree slopes on the other side of the ridge. They reached it after five hours' hard climbing. And there they now sat amidst this lunar landscape devoid of even a stalk of grass — they had unfortunately walked straight past the Alpine meadows. They took off their shoes and socks. Heinz S treated his injuries. Ms K felt dizzy. She wasn't hungry, just thirsty and thanks to Heinz S's foresight she even had a bottle of fresh spring water. He obviously did know what he was doing after all. They reckoned they would need another two hours to reach the next hut, where they planned to spend the night, only to be informed by some people they met after their rest that the hut chosen by Heinz S back in Cologne was not open that year because of staffing problems. They offered to take the pair of them to the nearest village by car after another hour's downhill slog. They declined, however. It would have meant starting right down at the bottom again on their third day. Nor could Ms K keep up with the pace set by the others since they had nothing to carry and were wearing much lighter shoes. So they soon lost sight of them. All the same, Ms K was pleased to hear about the unstaffed hut. It rather amused her. She was positively delighted by the fact that nothing had worked out up to now, despite all their preparations. Nevertheless, the prospect of possibly having to sleep outdoors and freeze, despite the sleeping bag, dismayed her just as much as the possibility of their still having to walk down to the next valley to the nearest inn. Ms K was glad he had insisted on the sleeping bag. Besides, she was struggling to keep going. She felt she was about to faint. They took a rest at the first cowshed that offered some shade. It was very hot. Heinz S spread out the Landjäger sausages that were sealed inside a plastic wrapping and swimming in some kind of cloudy liquid, his various kinds of salami, his tinned foods and different kinds of bread. Ms K pulled out the hundred gram bar of health food muesli concentrate she had packed. She decided to eat one of his sausages just to make his damned rucksack a bit lighter, at least symbolically, and to give him the feeling that he wasn't just carrying around rocks. It was pure mothering instinct. Ms K fished the Landjäger sausages out of their cloudy liquid and laid them on the stones to dry, amazed that anyone who cared about food could have gone and bought the things. The liquid was totally inconsistent with the very essence of Landjäger sausages which can be kept almost indefinitely precisely because they are dried. In all innocence and more interested in the underlying philosophy of such a purchase than anything else, Ms K thought they could spend the meal discussing certain errors of judgement that had been made. She found it all amusing and asked with affectionate irony what it was that made someone buy sausages for the mountains in Kleve knowing very well that (as they had seen in Merano) dried fruit and dried meat are local specialities developed for long distances and light luggage? Ms K had a vague idea that they would embark upon a lively discussion about all kinds of strange discrepancies. They might take his sausages to kick off with but Ms K had plenty of examples of her own to add. So she expected him to laugh and say something like, yes, he'd got as far as asking himself that too but he must have thought it such a good bargain at the time and sometimes when money just runs through your fingers in no time you suddenly start saving on the silliest of things etc. And then she would have said, exactly, that happened to her too, whenever she wanted to do something particularly well it always ended up in disaster.

But her friendly and altogether lighthearted question only made Heinz S's lips tremble and he totally lost his temper.

For God's sake, I've already said there was no time. What more am I supposed to do? Buy the crampons, my gear, I was running round all day to get all of this clobber. Isn't that good enough?

Ms K ignored his outburst. He was tired. So she suppressed an entirely innocently-meant remark about his having managed to buy the wrong crampons and, still hoping they might have a conversation, carefully pointed out that that was exactly what she meant. She just wondered why, even if he really did need these things, he had bought them there of all places. Apart from which he didn't have to justify himself, she wasn't attacking him in any way. It was more the principle that interested her, precisely because it was the sort of thing that happened to her too. There was no stemming the flow of words she used to placate him and prevent him from flying off the handle again. Nor was she complaining in any way, after all she was neither carrying nor eating the things . . .

She was always saying, 'I have to, he would have to', Heinz S retorted. He used to do that too, until someone had drawn his attention to it. He had steered clear of the phrase ever since. Then he bent down in the grass again and surreptitiously took a pill.

Indeed, Ms K had herself already noticed to her annoyance that she had been repeatedly telling him he didn't have to apologize for this, that or the other ever since he had picked her up in Munich two days earlier and she was growing increasingly weary of doing so. However, it wasn't the annoying aspects of her character that were under discussion at the moment. It was probably best for her to keep her mouth shut. And thus she buried any hope of having a pleasant exchange, a conversation. It all suddenly seemed very familiar. She decided she wasn't going to let anything spoil her good mood. She reached out for one of the now sun-dried Landjäger sausages and, as a peace-making gesture, for the bread too. It needed cutting out of its cellophane wrapping first and she was already holding the bread and the knife in her hands when he peremptorily demanded to have both at once and be quick about it. Not quite understanding what all this was about, she handed him the bread and the knife. But he didn't want them for himself at all. He wanted to be gallant and cut the bread for her. However, while doing so, he cut his finger badly. He almost cut it right off. Great spurts of blood gushed out of the wound. Ms K firmly told him to put his finger in his mouth and press on the artery while she scrambled around in the rucksack looking for the first-aid kit. Reluctantly he did as he was told. Ms K bandaged his finger but the blood soaked through straight away. She put on a second bandage and advised him to hold his finger up in the air. Heinz S was so shaken he was trembling and now it was his turn to feel as if he were about to faint. He was afraid he might get blood poisoning because the knife had been sticking in the ground. Ms K comforted him. He was bleeding much too profusely for there to be any danger of blood poisoning. Then she gave him the sugary muesli bars, one after the other, which he accepted gratefully with his uninjured hand. That consoled him.

He walked along in front of her again, holding his finger up in the air as if he were trying to test the direction of the wind all the time. His blisters made him limp. Now and then he would turn round quickly with a look of suspicion. And it suddenly dawned on Ms K that she was a threat to him. Men do not normally find themselves under observation. Her look was offensive quite simply because it was not dulled by economic or emotional dependence on the man walking along in front of her. And even when she had to stop looking at the scenery to concentrate on the route markers, and they actually managed to miss the path down to the village, which was to cause them no end of problems, her attention would still unexpectedly wander off in a new direction.

Ms K recalled what it had been like as a small girl to walk along behind her father — a man who was even younger then than Heinz S was now — at the mercy of the inexplicable behaviour of the grown-ups. She realized for the first time that the men she had once been so afraid of had been about thirty at the time. It was not her aged father who had inspired such terror but a relatively young man with a youthful face and a beautiful body. A man who would probably have beaten his wife had she dared ask him why he had gone and bought such-and-such a thing.

Heinz S was well-built but it was as if he were made up of two halves that didn't match. The erratic movements of the upper half of his body contrasted strangely with his evenly-paced and deliberate stride. His cut finger, his blisters, his idiotic purchases all seemed to make sense to her now. Ms K was overcome with affection and compassion. She suddenly realized what a complicated set-up each human being ultimately was. A person builds up an elaborate state of equilibrium and some other person who is trying to do the same misconstrues it completely and takes fright. At eighteen, she saw herself as a goddess to her own child. She of all people, she who was so fraught with shyness and feelings of inferiority she couldn't speak up for herself, complete a sentence or even walk along with her head up.

An elaborate system of clearly defined roles unfolded before her. One person establishes an image of strength and the other has to agree to uphold this façade or pay for it. Heinz S was right in sensing that Ms K had her doubts about whether he was as strong as he made out to be. What he didn't understand was that she didn't in the least demand it of him. In fact, he didn't really understand anything at all. He didn't have the option of just hitting out in helpless frustration. It was not in his nature, nor could he have reconciled such an act with his social conscience. But there was nothing to replace the behavioural void this left. Which is why he kept looking round at her with suspicion, for he was awfully vulnerable and quick to take offence. Perhaps he was right. Perhaps — set against the past two or three thousand years — it really was an act of heroism for a man to walk around in public with a woman who did not present herself erotically to him, nor did she work for him, nor was she dependent upon him in any way. Whatever the case, it was new to him and very hard going. He was clearly anxious for it to be recognized.

Plodding along behind him, Ms K reflected on the power of the weak and powerless. Irma Grewe came to mind, the young concentration camp warder who celebrated her twenty-second birthday in the autumn of 1945 during the Bergen-Belsen trial in which she was sentenced to death and subsequently hanged. Her thoughts turned to the women from Maidanek, charged in old age with crimes they had committed when they were young. And she thought of the Iranian Revolutionary Guards, fifteen-year-old boys some of them, with the power to check that women are wearing their headscarves properly, authorized to make arrests and who may even on occasion form the firing squads. She thought of the child soldiers in Latin America, drilled to hate and shoot and, once trained, capable of all kinds of bestiality. In the subsequent reports and analyses their deeds become those of 'fascist killer commandos'. The boys and youths that commit such deeds simply vanish by a trick of language. Abstract language is employed to nullify the horror or merely to simplify the problems to oneself. The term 'male violence' — yes, incredible though it may seem, it actually exists — is a fabrication of the same kind, reflected Ms K as she followed on behind Heinz S. All trace of the poor little wimps who commit the violence has been erased.

Heinz S felt as if he were under observation. Every time this feeling crept down his neck, he stepped aside to let her pass. He kept this up for five minutes at the most, after which he could no longer stand being behind her. Once, he tentatively put his arm around her. Ms K froze. She didn't like it. He couldn't accept that she didn't like it with the inevitable result that he was soon ranting on about how he had never yet met a woman so prudish that she wouldn't even let a guy put his arm round her. It just wasn't normal in his eyes. But the worst of it was that it made it more difficult for him to appear with her in front of others as a perfectly normal, respectable couple and not in some unseemly way as two people wandering around in the mountains together for some reason or other. As far as he and others were concerned, Ms K mused, it was preferable for her to be defined as a part of a respectable couple. Walking along beside him as a free individual, she was unsettling. Ms K did not feel tempted to correct his impression that she was a prude. She congratulated herself for having gone on this tour. She was quite unexpectedly encountering situations that led her to view familiar occurrences as if she were looking through the wrong end of a telescope except that she recorded her impressions dispassionately without being overcome by them. Ms K was not restricted by love. Or rather she was not restricted by fear, the fear that her observations would destroy his love.

Heinz S was beginning to like Ms K less and less. There was something wrong with her. His apologies suddenly seemed to belong to a bygone age. He began to find fault with her. Indirectly at first, grumbling about people who shrugged off harmless embraces, then carping about people who didn't go in for cooperating with others. Conceited, he called it.

Having her best interests at heart, however, Heinz S even went on to tell her that she couldn't possibly be happy the way she was living. Ms K had to laugh. God knows, there was no way you could say that. She rather maliciously asked him whether he was trying to imply that he could make her happy by putting his arm round her? Offended, he made no reply. Then, with a ring of triumph and revenge in his voice, he stated that she had nothing to gain by being so stand-offish. It wasn't even as if Ms K rejected him. She didn't dislike him by any means: she just preferred him at a distance, that was all. She only wished he would stop making those half-hearted gestures of his, but that was something he didn't understand. He'd never experienced what it was like to be on his own, she thought. He will always know how to protect himself from that. Indeed, not one of the men she knew knew what it was like to be on his own. She had once met a fifty-year-old man who had nodded away while a woman described her attacks of insufferable loneliness and claimed he knew all too well what she was talking about since he had been on his own once for four weeks as an eighteen-year-old student. She had witnessed the woman's jaw drop as the man went on about this for quite some time. Loneliness, thought Ms K, is an act of aggression. Loneliness is something so unaccepted that even those who live it hardly dare speak of it. It means you think yourself important, a thing others cannot tolerate. Heinz S had needed his girlfriend's reassurance, her endorsement of the trip. He would be lost without a girlfriend. Perhaps not without her as a person, Ms K suspected, but without her as an institution. For there was hardly a man who actually came to grief or turned over a new leaf after he'd been left. They nearly all immediately sought salvation in a new relationship. They cannot bear the sense of loneliness. Not to forget that it is the women who bring up these big babies, these drip-dependent men. They generally labour under the delusion that the attention they receive is meant for them personally, that the intimacy they experience is unique and non-transferable. But when it comes to the crunch they discover how wrong they are. Ms K said to herself: after losing a partner or separating, it's incredible how quickly a man can enter into a new, almost identical relationship with a woman who for her part also thinks that it has to do with her as a person and not what she stands for — to provide security.

They walked on and on, downhill all the time, but didn't seem to be getting much lower. They had lost their way. It was already growing dark when they met a farmer who offered the pair of them the hospitality of his house for the night providing they were 'respectable'. The farmer was an odd character, he might even have been a bit crazy but he was full of charm, generosity and dignity and had a gurgling laugh. The two men did not have very much in common. Heinz S tried to engage him in a discussion of the various maps, but the farmer wasn't interested, he 'knew the paths, you see'. He shrugged his shoulders, gurgled away and gazed at Heinz S as if he were some kind of strange animal. Heinz S was given warm milk fresh from the cow which cheered him up. Ms K

watched with disgust. Later they drank two bottles of wine
with the farmer who then showed them his private collection
of antiques which included old cow bells, tables and chairs,
none of which he was willing to sell, he gurgled. They both
hastened to say that they didn't intend to buy anything
anyway.

The next morning they made their way down into the
valley and put up at an inn. To keep up appearances as a
respectable couple they took a room together. At least the
beds hadn't been pushed right next to each other. By now Ms
K regarded their expedition as a kind of ethnological voyage
of discovery into unknown territory, which was why she did
not insist on a room of her own. On the contrary, she was
curious to know what surprises were still to come. They spent
the whole day sitting in one of the village meadows, resting.
Ms K sat in the sun reading a book, Heinz S sat up against a
fence a little way off in the shade trying to fit the crampons on
his boots. They had to find a new route which would allow
them to stay in the mountains without having to go up into the
High Alps. Conversation was slow. They ran out of things to
say unless she brought up a new topic. She knew he was
unhappy in his job and asked him to tell her about it. That
was just what he had been wanting to do. He had been
working himself to death and never received any thanks for it,
and now he was faced with having to decide whether to go on
with it or quit. It was 'all that lovely money' that stopped him
from quitting, he'd got so used to it. Making a fresh start
would be fraught with uncertainty and a great deal of stress.
Ms K tried to find out what he enjoyed doing but he grew
vague then. It was all tied up with his wanting to do
teamwork, to be involved in some kind of meaningful
communal activity. Ms K countered that clearly defined
interests were an absolute prerequisite for teamwork of that
kind. A person joining a project just for the sake of working

with others usually ended up by getting in the way of those who knew exactly what they were doing and why. Taking a chance, Ms K asked him what he had expected to get out of her. To her astonishment he immediately replied that he had hoped for a 'kick', a push in the right direction from her. Ms K flinched. The word totally confirmed the feeling that had been growing stronger and stronger inside her. He uncomplainingly carried all those salamis and tins of food because he expected her to give him something in return. She was being assessed. She would either be that 'kick' or she wouldn't. The scales suddenly fell from Ms K's eyes. This had nothing to do with hiking in the mountains as she had imagined. It was a business deal. Heinz S meanwhile had meant the bit about a 'kick' as a compliment and he was horrified by Ms K's reaction. It was becoming clearer and clearer — clearer and clearer to Ms K, that is. This was no confrontation between two people, it was the unresolved conflicts of centuries clashing head-on. They might as well have been speaking Chinese to each other. Heinz S had been paying her a compliment, in the way men always tell women they prefer the company of women — and, believe it or not, that was exactly what he went on to say. Women were the only people he could trust. Now it was a long time since Ms K had felt flattered by a statement like that. If only he had kept his mouth shut. She had learnt that the real reason for this revelation could always be traced back to fear and rivalry between two men. Never yet in her life had Ms K known any of the men who had made this confession to her reflect out loud in public what it was he was actually saying, which after all did have its consequences.

Heinz S cursed loudly for having ever uttered the word 'kick', at which Ms K could restrain herself no longer. She didn't resent his having expectations of her, she screamed. It was his refusal to make any effort that infuriated her. She had never been able to understand why people always dropped things as soon as they promised to get really difficult and had to play all these silly games instead. With the likes of him everything was fine as long as he could dictate the rules. One wrong foot and naked aggression came to the fore. He thought he was different just because he was a softie and had suffered at the hands of a man. All men thought they were different because all men suffered at the hands of other men. They seemed to hate each other so much, she continued, still screaming, that they could only establish their own integrity by dissociating themselves from other men all the time. Do I dissociate myself from every woman I don't like? Besides which and without making an issue of it, she now only had relationships with men who had a male friend as she had no intention of bearing sole responsibility for satisfying their emotional needs, and with men who could satisfy her that they had seriously thought about contraception. Not to mention sexuality. But unfortunately men like that just didn't exist. And, no, she certainly wasn't happy either. Shocked and hurt, Heinz S drew Ms K's attention to the fact that he hadn't said anything about another man. — No, said Ms K, but he was silently there with them all the time. She could only put up with the whole affair and see it through because she would be able to talk it over with her girlfriends afterwards. But even then she would still have to get round the added difficulty, one he would never have, of preventing other men who might hear about it from immediately dissociating themselves from the man she was talking about. That meant that, on top of everything else, she would be constantly preoccupied with protecting him from ridicule by other men. After all, it was hardly conceivable for a man to know something about another man and not turn it against him. Friendship between men, hah, that was nothing but an illusion. The best way she, Ms K, could protect him would be to keep her mouth shut altogether. She had honoured this tacit agreement for long enough but now she was no longer willing to guarantee that she would continue to do so. His way of defending himself was not, as one might expect, to confront those who might unfairly attack him, but to demand that she restrict her sphere of activity, thus requiring her to be masochistic. But if there was one thing she most certainly was not, it was a masochist. Men were simply in the embarrassing position of having to ask women to keep what they knew to themselves. His ancestors had certainly been on the right track in barring women from learning anything at all. That way they didn't have to stand in fear of their knowledge.

Heinz S stumbled as he began to realize that Ms K might spread the story of their hike and his needing a 'kick'. Of course, it went without saying that it was not a subject for gossip he said, while Ms K, still cursing loudly, asked more to herself than anyone else why it was that speaking out what you knew to be true was always taken as a hostile act that had to be suppressed. She by no means underrated the sanctions he could impose. But defensive weapons can be lethal too.

She didn't mean him any harm, she said in a conciliatory tone. What kind of 'kick' had he had in mind?

It was Heinz S's turn to be unresponsive now.

— You don't have to justify yourself.

— Stop saying, you don't have to.

— All right, I'm sorry.

— O.K., I'll tell you, I thought we might perhaps do some work together.

— Yes, but what kind of work? How can you be so sure that I'm the right person for what you want to do? My interests do go in rather a different direction or we'd hardly be quarrelling so much, would we? And then, laughing:

— You'll have your work cut out to convince me I need your help.

— You're so conceited.

— You'd have to put up with that if you want to work with me. Sorry, I mean, it would be necessary for you to put up with that.

And so it went on ad infinitum as if they had both taken leave of their senses.

Things were going steadily downhill and this was only day three. He had come to expect the worst from her by now. She could profess her good intentions to him as often as she liked, he wouldn't believe her. Her heart had been broken before and this was the same thing all over again. She was fed up with causing confusion all the time when she was only trying to be straightforward. Wherever she went, things polarized as if in a new system. The energies flowed differently. She could have promised him his 'kick' and forgotten the whole thing afterwards. That would have been all right, no breach of the rules. But, damn it, they weren't her rules.

They made an effort to be nice to each other during supper and even to conceal from each other the fatal impression they gave of a married couple with nothing more to say to each other. Ms K decided to make an effort to overcome this situation. She also decided to put a stop to her ethnological research. It would be a shame. He was a nice man. He bent down after each meal and took a pill. During a peaceful half hour after the evening meal Heinz S confessed to her that he was on psychoactive drugs, two different kinds his doctor had prescribed him. He had been feeling absolutely wretched for various reasons. Now she was the only other person to know about it apart from his girlfriend and his best friend. He was placing a lot of trust in her by telling her this. Apart from all this secretiveness about something he shared with at least five hundred million other people, and that was probably under-estimating it, Ms K was shocked at the trusting belief in the medical profession that enabled him to swallow the things.

She remembered the good deed a boyfriend of hers had done her years ago in taking her tablets away from her and suggesting she get to grips with her problems rather than swallow them away with a pill. She had been suffering from nervous strain and overwork at the time, with no hope of remedying the situation, and a doctor she had consulted had prescribed librium three times a day. She had taken the tablets just as obediently as Heinz S was taking his now, only to discover that they made her tired and she still had to do her work which was not getting any less. Summoning up her powers of persuasion, her knowledge of the subject and her sympathy for Heinz S, Ms K told him about the effect tablets had had in totally upsetting the lives of people who were very close to her. She told him about the effects of taking the pill, hoping that her persistence and friendship would at least sow the seeds of doubt about the beneficial effects of tablets of this kind and thus prevent the same experience from being repeated over and over again. Heinz S was not in the mood to hear any more about side-effects. He just wanted, so he said, to be happy for the remaining years of his life. The tablets were supposed to enable him to be just that. He was younger than Ms K but at that moment he reminded her of an old man. Nevertheless, in the next few days he began to give up taking the tablets but not without warning her of the dreadful consequences not taking them would have, like fits of depression and all the other side-effects listed on the leaflet in the packet. By the end of their trip he was down to taking just one tablet each time he became particularly annoyed with Ms K.

They stayed in the village for two nights, hardly moving at all for Heinz S's feet were looking a mess and now really did have to heal up properly. Heinz S rang his girlfriend in the evenings, able to reassure her that there was absolutely nothing going on between himself and Ms K. Ms K didn't ring anyone. Heinz S asked her who she had as her 'emotional prop'. Ms K almost choked at the word but managed to pull herself together. A minute later he was criticizing her for always having to go into 'the emotional side' of things.

— Yes, she said, how else can you communicate?

He didn't answer. He broke off the conversation. The only interesting thing left about him was his array of defence mechanisms, thought Ms K. But she remained friendly. Perhaps she told herself, I open up too much to everyone? Perhaps I should be more selective? But she didn't want to be more selective.

That evening, after she had finished telling Heinz S all she knew about the harmful effects of psychoactive drugs, Ms K took a tablet herself to help her to go to sleep in the same room as him.

On the fifth day they hitched to a new starting point. They could also have taken a bus but that was beneath Heinz S's dignity as a hiker. Tirelessly, he stood at the roadside watching car after car drive past and disappear. He had perked up visibly but Ms K was depressed by it all. In the end they were picked up by a married couple who were touring the valleys in a Mercedes. The woman drew her husband's attention to the beauty spots with a grunt and he would slow down as they drove past while she wound down the windows and took photographs from the moving car.

The plan was to take the cable-car up a particular mountain and to walk from there to the next hut. But the cable-car had broken down and would not be operating again for two weeks. Now that route was a washout too. And so, for the few days that remained, they decided to drive back to the village where they had parked their car and make short excursions from there — without their rucksacks which had not grown any lighter after all. Up to now they had really only had one day's hiking. That evening Ms K checked in at a small hotel and Heinz S slept in the car. He barely protested any longer. It didn't matter any more. Everything had gone wrong anyway. All the same, they still wanted to spend the next two days together and by tacit agreement they tried to get through them without quarrelling too much. Their problems wouldn't have been solved by curtailing the trip. After all, they basically wanted to remain friends. Their relations were like those between two superpowers undergoing a period of tension following the breakdown of arms control negotiations, during which diplomatic channels were used to let each other know that they had no intention of allowing the worst to happen.

They met at the village inn for a meal. Ms K asked him a question. Supposing she, Ms K, were a man, Alexander Kluge, for instance — whom he was carrying around with him in his rucksack in the shape of a paperback edition of *Learning Processes With Lethal Results* — supposing he and not she were hiking through the mountains with him, would he also accuse him of being uncooperative when he wanted to put his arm round him and the other didn't want him to?

The question was completely hair-brained as far as Heinz S was concerned for naturally he would never put his arm round a man. Ms K laughed and said that perhaps that was precisely their problem. He wasn't gay enough for her taste.

Of course he wouldn't put his arm round him nor expect anything of him either. After all, he would be walking alongside an intellectual genius.

— Aha.

And he wouldn't expect an intellectual genius to look after his emotional needs.

In that case, said Ms K, she suggested that he simply treat her as an intellectual genius and not expect it of her either. Then they could relax and might even have some real fun together. He wouldn't feel he wasn't getting his fair share any more then.

To quell his growing anger and inject some life into what had become a rather sparse conversation, Ms K asked him how he solved the problem of contraception with his girlfriend. She thought it a safe enough topic among friends. It had a lot to offer and was of general interest. She had already asked him the same question once before when they were waiting in the rain for the Castelbello train which was to take them back to their car but had not received a very satisfactory answer. He had said that was getting too intimate for his taste. Maybe he would answer it some other time. She'd have to make do with his telling her that his girlfriend didn't take the pill, which he respected, and he didn't like condoms. So, experienced as she was, she could work out for herself what method they used. She pondered over that it's something 'I respect'. As for the methods, she pictured a mixed bag of the calendar method, foams, pessaries, withdrawal, oral sex and masturbation. Or was Heinz S supposed to be sexually so enlightened that he made love according to the Tao of Love? She would have been envious of that but the longer she trudged along behind him, the less likely she considered it to be. After all, not only did he think she was repressed, she thought he was too. Now here she was sitting with Heinz S in Oberwirt repeating her question.

— What do you mean by 'respect'?

— Well, I respect the fact that my girlfriend doesn't take the pill although I'd be happier if she did.

— You'd prefer her to swallow some drug? Ms K could not quite suppress the desire to provoke him.

— It does have the desired effect, you have to bear that in mind too.

— In this case, I would say 'she has to'.

— What do you mean?

— After all, it's her liver, her water retention problem and her hair that falls out.

— Where have you got that from? It's all right for you to talk. And, my goodness, it's not as if I'm saying I demand it of her. The problem doesn't interest me.

— You try and keep up with the latest research where your work is concerned, don't you?

— Come on, there's nothing definite yet about the pill.

— Would you tell your girlfriend: It's all right, I quite understand about you not wanting to take an aspirin every day?

— But that's stupid.

— Sorry, I can't always be at my best.

His upper lip trembled. Ms K relented.

— We were talking about friendship between men just now, remember? You said you had friends with whom you discussed everything that's really important.

— Yes. He hesitated.

— Well, how do you and your friends discuss contraception, then?

— He stared at her in amazement. The dumpling almost fell out of his mouth.

— You haven't discussed it at all?

Ms K pretended to be genuinely surprised.

Heinz S sputtered out two short laughs, snorted and looked at Ms K suspiciously. He stopped eating and put down his knife and fork.

Then triumph gleamed in his eyes.

— You're right, I haven't discussed it. But I do know someone I could discuss it with.

Ms K suddenly felt the need for a change of tone. It was all so moralizing. What did it have to do with her. She decided to give the whole thing a humorous twist.

— You are now thirty-five years old. You've had, say, fifteen years' experience of sexual intercourse, right?

Heinz S nodded guardedly.

— Just about.

He thought it better to wait and see what was coming before committing himself.

— You're always saying you won't live to be an old man so let's say you've got the same number of years ahead of you at the most. Right?

He laughed.

— Or perhaps you won't die after all, but just become impotent in a few years' time. After all, it's supposed to happen to a lot of people in their mid-life crisis. But you don't smoke so you'll be up to it for a bit longer. Otherwise we'd have to knock off a few more years. What I'm trying to say is, it's about time, isn't it?

— Time for what?

— Time to discuss it with this man friend of yours, of course.

— Well yes, I suppose so. It's just never come up.

— No, it wouldn't have, said Ms K suddenly, more sharply than she had intended. It was only ever raised between women. They can say their hair is falling out because of the pill but it isn't something men friends talk about. At the most, you might say there's nothing definite. But it's not as if you make the slightest effort to prove the opposite. You never stop talking about fucking but there's not one of you that actually tries to find out the facts. I could imagine that your friends don't like condoms any more than you do. What do they do then?

— I've never asked.

— That's just it.

Ms K was fed up with herself and with him, too.

— Do you know how all this strikes me? I mean the whole thing. It's like someone being a declared anti-racist and all so proud of himself for opposing apartheid.

He was holding his knife as if he wanted to stab her right there and then.

For a few seconds she was scared stiff of him. They ate on in silence. What should they do. Two days to go. It would be such a shame. They would hardly be able to make up for defeat. It was a war of the species and hardly had anything to do with them as individuals. They both pulled themselves together.

She changed the subject. She was making a tremendous effort and would have deserved a medal for the work she was putting into their relationship. She tried to explain to him what the words 'cooperation' and 'harmony' triggered off in her. Various anecdotes entered her head by way of illustration. She related the first of them. A friend of hers is sitting in a coffee shop in San Francisco. A man accosts her and jostles her roughly. The other coffee-drinkers sit and watch without raising a finger. The man says: Are you married? Her friend answers angrily: That's none of your business. The man grabs hold of her and shakes her: Are you married, answer me! — That's none of your business! The man twists her arm, snatches her leather jacket from the chair and goes out. After a while he returns and snarls: I want to know because I don't mess around with married women. With that he left again. Taking her jacket with him.

Heinz S and Ms K ate their dessert in silence. She gave up the idea of telling him any more stories. His dilemma, she reflected, is that he'd do anything to avoid being mistaken for a patriarch yet he is unable to give up the privileges that go with it. The thought that women should be autonomous too was incompatible with his almost compulsive desire for harmony and togetherness.

— We can't just respond to ideas as such, says Ms K. We have to swallow them, digest them, and wait and see what happens.

She could understand his anger and the way he played on her fears and her cowardice, which she herself yielded to often enough anyway, rather than following her curiosity and instinctive desires.

— Why have you stopped talking? Heinz S wanted to know after a while.

— Out of desperation, she said.

After that, they went to bed. He in the car, she in the hotel. On the way back Heinz S chivalrously walked along beside her on the dangerous side next to the road, and in doing so half pushed her into the ditch, causing her to stumble several times. Ms K surreptitiously wiped away a tear.

They went on short excursions for the rest of the time. Without their rucksacks. In light shoes and each with a book in their hand. They were already thinking of the time after their return. The enterprise had failed. What was it that had gone wrong?

He manages to make me feel like a monster, she thought.

What dreadful repression of her aggressive instincts stopped her from telling him what she thought. Or was it consideration? Why was she always defending him? She drove him to distraction. If only he knew how much she was keeping herself in check.

— It's not as if I'm rejecting you because I think I can do everything better on my own. I yearn to be able to work together with others. I'm well aware of my limits. I want to be loved too. But not at the cost of compromising myself. All I hear all day long is that there's something wrong with me. Too true, there's something wrong. There was a guy once, some time ago now, to whom I made the greatest declaration of love in my life. I wanted us to work together. But what for me was just the beginning, the groundwork, the area to be covered to clarify my own doubts was already the last lap as far as he was concerned. Later on this guy wanted us to get together again and said, my work is ticking over nicely on its own now, if you know what I mean. I can do it automatically. Everything's running smoothly with you too, I hope.

As this last remark gradually sank in, I knew it was true, we just didn't belong together. It takes Mach 1 to break through the sound barrier. It would take at least Mach 4 to get through to this man. It was the concept of work being done on its own, automatically, that did for me. There's only one kind of work I know anything about, it takes luck, application and peace and quiet for you to finally catch a glimpse of the clarity you would like to achieve. It's like using a hammer and chisel to bring out what is potentially in a piece of stone but which appears only once the work has been done.

But you can still get me down with your pedantry, you know. You'd be quite capable of doing that. All I can say is that if I have one aim in life it's to hold out against you and the likes of you. I'm so glad I resisted your vision of happiness. But it hurts to hear you say I'm waging war. I can tell you. I long for peace and harmony too, you know. It came to me again only last night. There was this young man roaring through the village on his souped-up motorbike for hours on end, making as much noise as possible. From ten o'clock at night to two in the morning, to be precise. The village was so small, he screamed past my window every four minutes. This young man was terrorizing the whole village but there was not a soul there to stop him from doing so. And should I unexpectedly prove to be tough after all, and you men don't succeed in crushing me, there's the role of demon woman you've invented for me. But I wouldn't want to become cynical, even if I live to be a hundred and seventy. If I were a man you'd know that I've spent years thinking about sexuality and fertility. If I were a man you'd have nominated me for the Nobel Prize had you been able to. And yet you have the gall to say that contraception doesn't interest you and still rabbit on about how important cooperation is. You wouldn't be so proud of your ignorance if you were talking to a man. With a man you'd feel inferior if you didn't know the facts. And if cooperation were really so important to you, you'd have put some effort into it, done your research and dug up the information. You'd have tried to become an expert. But you're in the best of company. As far as men are concerned, it's no mark of inferiority to know nothing about women's ideas and their achievements but in our day and age it most certainly is to know nothing about the conflicts in Nicaragua or South Africa. They'd be ashamed of themselves if they didn't have at least a rough idea about gene technology. No matter which side they supported, they'd never dream of viewing internal party disputes as anything other than an honourable and conscientious attempt on the part of all concerned to come to grips with real on-going conflicts. Inasmuch as they are in possesssion of any facts at all, they'll do their utmost to use their knowledge to influence things. They'd never dare, as they do on the question of women, to consider themselves well-informed on the strength of the little they've gleaned from reading one or two paperbacks over a period of several years. But you have the audacity to do exactly that when it comes down to women's lib, Ms K continued, even though it has already changed your life more than you realize.

— You're even proud of your ignorance. You want praise and a pat on the back for what should be taken for granted.

Their last morning had arrived. Heinz S drove Ms K to the Post bus. Ms K intended to visit a friend of hers in Switzerland for a few days. They drank a final cup of coffee together. Heinz S advised her not to travel around too much during the next few weeks, it would be too much for her to take in. Then he went on to say that she was authoritarian. Ms K couldn't believe her ears. So it seemed there was something vital she still hadn't understood. She had slept in his car, she had thumbed a lift, which she hated doing, she had followed the routes he had chosen, she had respected his experience, stuffed her rucksack according to his instructions. But he probably only thought she got on his nerves with her questions. As a parting shot, he said with a sly and triumphant expression on his face:

— I'm only glad I didn't tell you anything about myself. You put the bar up high but I slipped through underneath it.

That evening Ms K is sitting with her friend in Switzerland. She tells her about the hiking holiday and the other woman picks up the thread, embellishes on it and they laugh. My God, how they laugh together. As chance had it, they were joined by another woman. The stories grow wilder, the laughter louder.

Back in Cologne, Ms K tries to ring Heinz S twice, three times. His girlfriend always answers the phone. Ms K would like to meet them both and pick up the one or two things she had left behind in his car. His girlfriend would like to meet her too. But Heinz S never rings back. One day he rushes up to Ms K's flat with the things she had forgotten, thrusts them into her hands and disappears, all within the space of twenty seconds. — I'll give you a ring. That was it for the next few years.

TALKING AMONG THEMSELVES

The Ms K who had been telling this story sniffled. In fact, she was having a little weep. The second Ms K gave her a handkerchief. An old-fashioned man's handkerchief made of cloth. It had a brown border woven into the material and a monogram. Ms K took it and looked at it with such surprise that she forgot her sniffling.

— She's just used to crying in better circles, that's all, the pregnant one said flippantly.

— You can see how hard it is for me to keep control of myself all the time, the middle one said apologetically.

— Or how much they make you cry.

— That's true. I've got at least fifty like that. A whole pile from PW. And from GS, of course. That's the biggest pile of all. And a few odd ones, too.

— I always use Softies, the first one said with a certain contentment and vigorously blew her nose on the mono-grammed handkerchief.

They all three looked with interest at the handkerchiefs that the second one pulled out from one drawer or another.

— They just accumulate as time passes, the third one said philosophically.

— I know a JR too, the first one shrieked pulling a blue-bordered handkerchief towards her with her knitting needle.

— Hands off, said the second one. To each her own Jay Ar.

— We could make a patchwork quilt with them, fill it with down, all snuggle down under it and never wake up again, said the third.

She regarded her knitting critically, a scruffy half-finished sleeve which, as they all could see, would never make a nice pullover.

The second one produced the letter she had received that morning.

— I've got a holiday story too, she said.

A HOLIDAY LETTER

I'm sitting sheltered from the wind on the small terrace of my one-room bungalow, looking out onto dunes and other bungalows and writing you this letter.

Every now and then someone passes by. In the last two or three years, these few visitors have already spoiled the beach, so I've been told, and completely transformed life here. Here, in the land of the 'dirty Arabs' (they have called us 'Stinkers' since the days of the Crusades), the 'Keep the Place Tidy' fanatics we know at home litter the sand with their empty tins of sun cream and orange peel. The waste bins that have been provided are hardly ever used. Now and then I come into conversation with people who have travelled halfway round the world on some package tour or other. They compare the prices of a week in Majorca with a week in Ceylon, Thailand or Greece. The price differential becomes a country's main distinguishing feature. A cheap country rates well. Tunisia is considered acceptable.

As soon as it gets a little warmer bare-breasted women lie on the beach or beside the hotel swimming pool in the midday sun. Five hundred metres away, veiled Arab women stand at the roadside in their yashmaks, which only ever leave one eye uncovered, holding them between their teeth when they need both hands free. They nearly always need them free for their children and the many plastic bags they carry. On the beach, Arab youths hire out horses or camels by the hour. When I go for a walk on my own — as I do for one or two hours every morning to keep fit — they and other men who appear out of the dunes regularly accost me. There have been one or two occasions when I have shouted and sworn at these men. But that is something I can only risk doing as long as it is light and there are people in the vicinity. I've come to realize this and now adopt tactics that are effective twenty-four hours a day. On two occasions I have explained my position in French to two of the youths, they must have been about eighteen. Would they please for once in their lives try and imagine how they would feel if they had to put up with someone talking to them, following them or walking alongside them at least ten times along a stretch of beach just five kilometres long. Every day. They both stared at me in astonishment, laughed with embarrassment and apologized. They promised not to do it again. Now I sometimes see them in the distance and they give me a conspiratorial wave of the hand. They are so naturally assured of their male superiority they are able to treat me with grandiose generosity.

Many of them are just trying to be friendly when they make their advances or walk along beside you. That's something I've learned too. They're just as accustomed to greeting people today as our villagers back home were decades ago. At any rate, I've given this act of greeting or not greeting, of smiling or scowling a good deal of thought and it is far more important than the casual observer might think when he or she sees a young man and woman meet in the distance. In the evening I prefer not to rely on the effectiveness of my powers of persuasion. So I stay indoors, and just lie on my bed on my own. Of course, there's something to be said for this too. While others watch the so-called entertainers encouraging the cobras or scorpions to dance, I have time to let my thoughts wander, read a book and wonder how these boys can be expected to cope, caught between the semi-naked females they meet as tourists and the veiled women at home. There's a night watchman too, employed by the hotel management to patrol round the bungalows for burglars. He's armed with a thick club and wrapped in the local desert garb, a rough, thickly-woven burnous with a hood. You wouldn't want to meet him in the dark or in the daytime either.

The women who lie there topless in the sun with their 'New Woman' paperbacks in their bags and protected by their men in their European pair-units, have no idea of the damage they are doing. It seems to me that there is a direct link between their nakedness and the fact that I get chatted up. They won't notice it until their men have deserted them. I enjoy feeling the sun on my skin too but what once began as liberation back home is seen as an insult here. The barkeeper feels insulted because I don't want to sleep with him even though he 'made me the offer'. He thought that that is the way European women amuse themselves. 'A different mentality,' he called it.

There's something cowardly about stripping here in the Tunisian hotel zone. They wouldn't do it a hundred kilometres down the coast in Gaddafi-land. Not so long ago an eleven-year-old girl was beaten to death there for riding a bicycle in Bermuda shorts. German and American barebreastedness irritated me enough in Italy. The little kids they had in tow had to advertise their parents' ideology by running around naked. They would be stripped completely not only on the beach, where the little Italian girls all wear bikini tops, but taken onto the promenade naked too just to show the Italians how backward they are. And then you can experience new variations in family horror as the local population stares in astonishment: Man with a beard, in baggy jeans, of course, sandals and woollen socks, or, worse still, shorts and woollen socks. This combination of woollen socks and sandals appears to be the hallmark of the German male. Seriously, what do we do to encourage it? It's so widespread that somehow we must have wanted it that way. Dad will proudly show off his beer belly, if he can, and I'd rather not get started on Mum.

The topless women tourists, perhaps even women in swimsuits, make it impossible for Tunisian women to go onto the beach. I don't know if they used it themselves before we came. I only know that local women can't be found on the beach now. I noticed this because today, after being here for two weeks, I saw an exception. She was veiled and accompanied by her husband to a warm spring where Arab men in bathing suits were lying in the pools. The woman stood a little to one side and looked the other way. When you see Arab women out with their husbands, they outwardly demonstrate their social relationship. They walk along behind them. European couples make a show of their emotional relationship. When they're on holiday they usually make a point of demonstrating INTIMACY. They will walk along holding hands or kiss each other in public when they're in love while couples who have known each other longer will sometimes hold hands too and walk along in silence. Surrounded as I am by a hundred couples inside and outside the hotel, there's something that distinctly attracts me about the way the Arabs stress the difference and strictly segregate the sexes. Of course, the women are oppressed and it is extremely embarrassing to witness a scene in which a woman is knocking on the inside of a door so that the man can open it from the outside, take something from her and then sell it to me. To the woman, whose glance momentarily meets mine, I am suddenly conniving with the man. I wear long-sleeved blouses now when I take the bus into town so as not to offend the women. I can see that they register the fact by the look in their eye, in the one visible eye of the veiled women, and because they don't shrink back inwardly as they do when a sleeveless, bra-less and sockless European woman gets on.

In the medieval atmosphere of the Moorish baths I visited, the women had great fun. I had discovered them by accident and enquired whether I would be admitted too since they were in a purely Arab area out of the way of the tourist quarter. They were open for men in the mornings and women in the afternoons. The women would frolic around performing feats of great skill with their invariably enormous breasts, making them wobble and dance amidst the laughter of all. They all looked like the 'Willendorf Venus'. I was flabbergasted. They were too, but for a different reason. The black woman who bathed and massaged me ran her hands over my body dubiously. She had never seen such a thin woman before. To be on the safe side, she fetched her colleagues, all of them black. They fingered me one after the other and appeared to be debating whether I would survive the treatment. We made signs to each other to convey what it was that most amazed us both, their large breasts and my small ones. We were probably laughing about the same things when we laughed. Incidentally, everyone keeps their pants on in these baths. Strict prudery is the rule. But the women who bathe the others pour water out of tin cans over the women's bellies and legs, pulling away the elastic a long way as they do so. Later, I saw some of these women again sitting stoically and silently in the bus with their yashmaks covering their mouths and one eye. I only recognized them by the small distinguishing features of their yashmaks which I had noticed earlier in the baths when I was able to examine them while they were hanging on the hooks in the decorative blue mosaic restroom.

My being so curious and considerate has probably only made me an advance party for hordes of tourists who will be offered the baths as a new attraction next year making it impossible for the local people, or at least the local women, to go there.

The Arab waiter I met on the beach told me that he would never marry a Tunisian woman, they 'weren't clever'. When I protested he explained that they might have compulsory education but, all the same, the girls were usually kept at home after two years at school and forced to work. (I, too, have seen the young girls making carpets.) He intends to enable his eleven-year-old sister to finish school. He is eighteen and can speak five languages passably well. But that won't get him very far.

Asociality is perhaps a better word than imperialism. Imperialism no longer implies individual responsibility. The word mystifies barbaric conditions as the product of an abstract concept of capitalism. Imperialism is the modern version of the devil who's never inside you but always inside the others. But here in Tunisia it isn't just the big foreign companies that are destroying the country. It even follows a non-aligned foreign policy and there are no Americans here. It's the millions of little crimes, none of them indictable as such, that cause immediate destruction, and the tourist piranhas appear to be completely insensitive to the asociality of it all. We're imperialists merely by virtue of the fact that we're here in droves, however poor we may be at home, and not the other way round. They, the Tunisians, don't flock to Pasing or Passau or Heidelberg. They can't afford to ask the women tourists to dress decently please, decently by their standards. You can capitulate in the face of reality or even make an issue of it, if you can visualize the clash, the confrontation between a poor and chauvinistic Arab boy and a militant, but self-righteous European lesbian railing against male violence. But what's all this about 'the Tunisians'? This isn't about Tunisian women. It's the Tunisian men who have the say. So it's not as if I were in favour of slavishly observing foreign habits and customs for they are seldom in the interests of the women, that's for sure.

So you see, dear K, it's not at all easy to relax properly.

The most ridiculous things happen in a hotel like this. A German hotel guest will probably go to court for the following reason. Having brought along his thermometer from home, he discovers that at night the temperature in his bungalow drops to fifteen degrees. According to the brochure it should be eighteen degrees. He demands his money back. People drive out into the desert and return safe and sound only to complain at suppertime that they had to wait two hours for a bus even though the guides and tour organizers had warned them beforehand that delays were to be expected. One woman shed seven pounds on her visit to the Berbers! Why? Because they had to get out of the bus at some point and climb up a mountain, not even a proper path, to reach the place where the Berbers lived. They're all within their rights. The one I like best is a Swabian woman who gets frightfully upset about all the poor people who have to live here surrounded by 'nothing but sand' (which she says in a broad Swabian accent). She was sitting behind me in the bus on our excursion to a village of cave-dwellers distributing the sandwiches she had had the foresight to make to two men who were staying in the same hotel. The Arabs have obviously not kept abreast of the times, emotionally speaking. But they will probably learn quickly. You still get the impression that they really mean you when they smile at you, that they have unlimited reserves to draw on. The tourists are obviously a mystery to them but they remain polite. Perhaps this is all that remains of the sacred tradition of honouring a guest. However hot it may be, the waiters line up before serving, impeccably dressed, jackets and all, and watch without a flicker as the men and women, many of them still dressed for the beach, take their seats at the tables. As a rule, their table manners are disgusting. The majority make a mad dash for the cold buffet that is served daily as an hors d'oeuvre as if they never got enough. There's always plenty there. On one occasion, a magnificent buffet was served as the main course for the evening meal. It almost ended in a fight. People were grabbing the dessert, delicious

Tunisian cakes, at the same time as the hors d'oeuvres just to make sure that they didn't miss out on anything. Not just one or two, but five or six at a time. Don't they know how much they can eat or is it just pure greed? Later, they would sit there with their mouths full, choking on the mountains of cake they had piled up on their plates only to leave much of it as an unsightly mess. Many of them were sick afterwards. I'm so immune to the lure of holiday thrills because I relate this rush and grab at the buffet to the sex-life that probably goes with it. My stomach turns at the thought and I close up like a clam. I'm chronically het, as you know, but even so I can't find a single object of desire.

The man who sat next to me at the table for a week and knew the hotel well, having spent several winters there, told me that the boiled eggs used to be placed in baskets for everyone to serve themselves at breakfast. Now you have to order them separately and state your room number because people used to fill their bags with them and take them down to the beach for their picnics. It's the same with the ashtrays. They're only cheap Tunisian pottery but they look pretty. More and more guests have arrived since I've been here and every day more of the ashtrays disappear. Now they are being replaced by ugly ones made of pressed glass. The generosity that people have found so enchanting here is being destroyed by greed. The guides point out the sights and the tourists pour out of the buses, cameras at the ready. Whether it's on video or super-8, they all take pictures of their wives at the side of a man in a burnous who has been instructed to put his arm round her, and you have that nasty feeling that they are 'immigrants out' supporters back home. If the Arab wants money for having his photo taken, they shower him with abuse. The most interesting pictures would probably be the other way round, with the locals taking photographs of the tourists.

Do you remember that we could hardly believe it when we heard that they were developing medicines to cure depression, back in the fifties? We imagined how concentration camp survivors would be given pills to combat their grief. We get a shock sometimes watching the films they made then, seeing the actors sitting at a breakfast table in the middle of a real meadow. A meadow full of the kind of flowers that you haven't seen in a meadow for ages, you realize. Or you see a film in which the actors walk freely over the tarmac to climb into an aeroplane without being protected, or threatened, by police with machine-guns, without first going through a security scanner and being searched, and without people carrying those disgusting sandwich packs, some of them even taking two just because they're free. How I hate that. And how I hate to see them eat the lot before the flight has even started. I could understand it if it tasted nice, but you wouldn't want to eat that junk unless you were dying of hunger.

That's more or less the kind of shock I get when I meet up with young couples in their twenties at the hotel. They've obviously grown up on a diet of Sesame Street, package tours and comprehensive education and, instead of doing something more exciting or, at least, something different like showing a spark of curiosity about the place they happen to be in, they submit to the hotel regime as if it's the most natural thing in the world. You can't even blame them for being the dull and dreary people they've been made into. They will have had to work hard enough for their holiday. They listen to me, eyes wide in amazement, when I tell them about my trips out into the desert. It simply never occurs to them that they could be doing something else instead of just lying around on the beach or by the swimming pool. But even if my stories do sometimes prompt them to think about doing something on their own initiative it all comes to nothing when they realize they might miss the lunch they have already paid for. They're afraid that someone, like the tour operators, might be making a profit out of them if they go off by themselves and miss a meal for once. They'd have to pay for an extra meal then. It just doesn't occur to them that they could skip a meal. Or they could ask for a packed lunch.

I'm a package tourist myself but I'm more like some kind of fossil that has accidently got caught up in the arrangements all the others appear to accept so easily. You can bet your life on it, I'm sure to be the one they single out for a customs check. I'm like my aunt who's almost eighty years old. She's never given up dreaming of the independence she has never really had and shows it by waiting at the traffic lights while they turn red and green and red and green again only to cross the road when she happens to feel like it and not as dictated by the lights. This is the same aunt who, quite out of keeping for an old lady in the Federal Republic and long before punk arrived on the scene, used to stick gaudy combs and beads in her hair 'because, who knows, my dream man might still come along one day'.

Dear K, that's enough for a goodnight story. But I'm staying here for another week so it's quite possible a second might follow. That's the way it is; our fear of going out at night and the boredom of what we find if we do, our dread not of the desert, but the dreariness, makes us gradually grow wiser. There's dialectics for you. Give my love to your Ms Ks. Affectionately yours.

MS K WATCHES ANOTHER WOMAN

Ms K is spending the Christmas holidays at a small hotel in a remote mountain village with her much younger boyfriend whom tactless people mistake for her son. They've booked half-board. There is no other restaurant in the village. On the very first evening she notices a woman sitting on her own at the next table. She's not expecting any one else, only one place has been set. The hotelkeeper had asked the lady whether she had managed to get some rest and she had nodded, lying as Ms K could see. She could swear she'd seen her somewhere before. She is very attractive and has an enormously conspicuous bosom. She is wearing a plain dark-blue zipped sweater. It must be either ages old or very expensive or from East Germany. Ms K is surprised to see this woman here in this village at this time of year. It doesn't fit. But perhaps it does fit after all, she corrects herself quickly. She doesn't tell her boyfriend how fascinated she is by the woman at the next table but makes an excuse to change places with him so that she has a better view of her. The other woman picks up the brochures that are lying around and reads them from cover to cover. Then she reads the menu. She is endeavouring to appear occupied although she knows that everyone else is occupying themselves with her. She drinks rather a lot of wine. The most expensive sort. She smokes. She asks for a newspaper but the hotel doesn't have any.

Ms K suppresses her impulse to ask the other woman to join them at their table. That would have been the worst thing she could do. After all, she had picked up this young man of hers in time for Christmas to avoid being in exactly the same position herself. But really, she admits to herself in the next breath, this flippant observation was only an attempt to protect herself, to avoid an attachment that was bound to end in tears — her tears, of course. For her boyfriend is young and naturally she mustn't cling to him. After all, he had to experience things for himself and learn what life was all about.

And yet on the face of it, things look quite different for the time being, and Ms K is occasionally moved by this deception and quite happy to play along with it for a while. When he told her that he loved her she asked him if he could be more specific. He replied that he loved her because she was beautiful, intelligent, unconventional and because he so infinitely enjoyed sleeping with her. To be even more specific, he said after a while: 'I need you.'

At that moment Ms K would have liked one of her friends to be there so she could ask her whether she'd ever heard of a woman saying 'I need you' to a man without him running off immediately.

The next day Ms K remembers who this woman is. A rather well-known journalist with a profound knowledge of history who specializes in the economic history of Asia and Africa. She is renowned for her sharp tongue which would come as a surprise to anyone seeing the hotelkeeper's rather condescending attitude towards her and her somewhat shy response to it. She is also the mother of several grown-up children, she's even supposed to be a grandmother, and years ago she had a reputation on account of her love affairs. Ms K suddenly knew how the other woman had landed up at this table. She wanted some peace and quiet but had not been able to make her arrangements in time. There was a practical and a nostalgic reason for her not being able to do so. The practical reason was that something always crops up at the last minute when you work freelance and, to judge by her own experience, anyone who thinks they can take advantage of cheap off-peak air or rail fares or any of the other special offers invariably ends up by paying twice, once for the unused cheap ticket and again for the new ticket that has to be bought at the normal price. She did not have the house in the country that most of her colleagues had acquired by now. Her money had gone on the children. In a large hotel at a winter resort she would have met too many people she knew and she wouldn't have had the energy to justify or transcend the fact that she was alone and, in either case, endure being an object of curiosity. She hoped no one would recognize her in a little village, yet she'd be protected there and able to rest and regain her strength. She had pictured a pleasant room in an old-fashioned inn somewhere off the beaten track where they served good plain food instead of your standard oriental rice dish and Hawaii Toast. She'd been way off the mark there and that had to do with the second, the nostalgic reason for her being there. She'd been done often enough in the past, but she still hadn't been able to resist the temptation of driving off 'into the blue' — the blue, that captivating figment of her imagination that had formed in her mind before the days of mass tourism. Ms K works as an editor in a large publishing house and as such she is extremely well versed in the literature on the subject. She can see the books in front of her: *The Green Hell of the Amazon*, for instance — all adventure and existentialism. That's why she was wearing the sweater and the long scarf. She had probably not been able to find a hotel at the first place to catch her fancy, let alone a single room at a time like this during the festive season when even doubles were in short supply. She was not brave enough to rent an isolated well-heated hut up in the mountains and enjoy the pleasures of television with remote control, Scotch and music, Ms K reflects sympathetically. The upshot of this youthful dream of

just 'driving off anywhere' is that here she is sitting in this
dreary hotel that isn't even cheap, being treated with a sneer
because she is on her own. Ms K hears other people gossiping
about how 'that woman' had paid extra for the double room
because the single room had been too small for her. Not only is
she paying more, she's giving herself a bad name too. The
hotelkeeper openly debates whether she is respectable, on
account of the double room, and, besides, self-assured women
travelling alone are always suspected of being terrorists. The
local police keep a discreet eye on her. In brief, she's a public
outrage and it takes a lot to endure that. Being a public
outrage is just about as hard as being a beauty. The most
difficult thing about it is surviving the High Church holidays.
Ms K sketches a domestic scene on her serviette, a table, a sofa
and television, a dot, twigs hung with Easter eggs and a
woman.

— What is it? she asks her boyfriend.

He doesn't know.

— A woman with a fly, on her own in her flat at Easter,
answers Ms K laughing heartily on her own. Her boyfriend
stares at her blankly and Ms K pulls herself together. She tells
her boyfriend the story of how she could have had the use of a
colleague's cottage. She would have loved to have rented it.
She had spent one night there and been terrified. It was miles
away from anywhere. She had wondered whether she would
be able to get used to it there. She quite probably would have
but she would never have been able to relax. And yet the
cottage was ideal. It had a garden, it was well laid out, it was in
good condition, it wasn't kitsch, it was cheap and it was easy
to get to. But she was afraid and didn't want to have a guard
dog. A young male colleague of hers was living there now.

— I would have loved to move in with you, her boyfriend says.
Ms K stares at him, overwhelmed by a wave of emotion. She
can well understand why older men fall for younger women.

The young can be so breathtakingly heartwarming with their smoothness, their soft downy cheeks and those bright eyes of theirs.

Ms K tells her boyfriend another story, lowering her voice so that the other woman can't hear her and won't think she is talking about her. Ms K recounts how she had been looking for a hotel in a small town in Italy one evening without finding one. She hadn't booked in advance. When she said 'without finding one' what she meant was that she had spent two hours that evening going round to every bloody hotel in the place, no matter what category, and been followed by two men all the time who had been offering her one thing after another if only she would go with them. She ran to the station in the end, it was already half-past midnight by that time. She was lucky. A train with a sleeper pulled in and there was even a bed free. It was still very early in the morning when they arrived at the train's destination. There, in Livorno, she found the most expensive hotel there was, booked a luxury suite for one night and went straight back to bed. Her boyfriend now looks rather disapproving, he's probably thinking of her credit card.

Evenings descend quickly in winter. Supper is served between seven and half-past. The hotel is dead after that. After supper, Ms K goes for a walk through the village with her boyfriend. The only other bar, the Blue Hawaii, in which they have something to drink, closes at half-past nine too. Ms K glances out of the window and thinks she can see 'that woman' walking past.

When they return to the inn, the light is on in the journalist's double room. Ms K imagines she is probably lying in bed reading a detective novel. The rooms don't even have a television. For a fleeting moment Ms K envies the other woman her detective novel. She hasn't got round to reading hers yet.

You have to have what it takes to stick it out in these rooms. It's impossible to escape the enforced intimacy. This makes Ms K uncontrollably aggressive. Her boyfriend doesn't mind it so much. He clowns about and even makes her laugh for a while. Their room consists of a double bed and a built-in wardrobe. There's a shower and a toilet in an open alcove next to the bed. On the other side, there's a small gap between the bed and the window with a patch of carpet on it. Ms K flushes with anger at the stinginess of the hotel proprietors who unashamedly divide up rooms that are too small anyway so as to squeeze even more rooms and hence more money out of the building. Ms K is lying in bed next to the young man, feeling a stranger to herself. She is annoyed that she has agreed to stay in this wretched place miles away from anywhere. They converse in whispers and move quietly because the walls are thin. And yet it had been difficult enough to find anywhere at all at such short notice. She couldn't take advantage of the special offers expensive hotels also make for those who can commit themselves early enough. They're not even more expensive then, just nicer than this stuffy joint in which the two of them are now lying under the covers. She had been thinking of him. She didn't want to offend him and pay for him. Although that was something of a con, as she was paying for him to give her skiing lessons which she didn't really need and he was financing his stay that way. Whatever the case, she wouldn't have had the money to pay for the two of them to stay at a grander hotel anyway. But if she were to book in the spring, who can guarantee that she'll still be with her boyfriend by the time winter comes round? She longs to be back home in her own bed.

The next morning she looks out of the window to see the other woman walking across a broad open space. She's heading for the next village and bracing herself against the wind. There are two paths, a long and monotonous one across this white expanse and an interesting one through the forest. If she were alone, she'd go across the open country too, Ms K says to herself as she turns contentedly towards her boyfriend who is still asleep.

That afternoon Ms K is just about to enter the chemist's when she discovers the journalist inside and tactfully stays outside. Ms K starts rummaging around in her handbag in search of something and, looking in a mirror, she sees what she had suspected might be the case — the other woman is buying sleeping tablets. They nod to each other briefly as 'the woman' leaves the shop and Ms K and her boyfriend go in. They meet again later in a bookshop in another town that is famous for its café and delicious cakes. The only books displayed on about twenty rows of shelves in the bookshop are all published by Heyne. But it is a normal bookshop. Why do they only sell books by this one publisher? the woman editor asked in amazement.

The assistant answered that these were the only books that were the right height for the bookshelves. They had bought the shelves along with the shop from the previous owner and it had turned out that the other books were too big. Hereupon, the two smile at each other for the first time. Ms K promises to give the woman journalist a detective novel because she won't get round to reading it. And they both glance briefly at the young man who is outside helping a small boy with the clasps on his skis. Then they turn away from each other quickly.

The small hotel fills to bursting for New Year's Eve. The hotelkeeper ushers the single lady to a table where both younger children and teenagers are seated. These six youngsters had been sent there by their intelligent parents for a week on their own. They ski all day and romp around in their rooms all evening until the knocking on their walls forces them to quieten down. The woman protests. She doesn't want to sit at the same table as the children. She wants

to sit on her own. She is saying this on principle now, to show
that she can't be pushed around. But she is less firm than she
would have liked to have been, after all she has nothing
against children and, of course, she doesn't really want to sit
on her own. But she wants to be treated with respect and that
means not being seated next to the children. Yet the table she
had previously regarded as hers has been taken by a couple
that has just arrived. Nevertheless, the woman's wish is
respected, and she is given a small table that is placed right
between the doors to the toilets and the kitchen. Everyone is
watching. The woman now sits there hidden behind a large
newspaper, *Die Zeit*, which she has bought because it takes a
long time to read and it's large enough to hide behind. But
after a while she would like to move from here too. If it weren't
for the snowstorm she'd probably pay her bill and leave.

The tables have been specially laid for New Year's Eve.
New candles have been placed on the tables. Only at this
woman's table has the tiny stump from the previous day been
replaced by another stump from the neighbouring table, one
that was not quite so small. With a slight tremor in her voice,
the woman says she would like a new candle too. Then she
says she would like to sit with the children after all. But that is
no longer possible, other arrangements have been made at the
table by then. Under no circumstances was she going to stay
next to the toilet, she said. This in a new tone of voice. In the
end, she is given a place at a table next to a married couple and
their child. This is not without psychological subtlety on the
part of the hotelkeeper. To this small family unit the woman is
a truly interesting and welcome addition in a way she would
not have been for the couples at the other tables. There is
hardly a table at which people are not whispering about her
and her big bust. Even Ms K's boyfriend suddenly announces
he thinks he's seen the woman somewhere before. But Ms K
doesn't follow it up. She safeguards the woman's anonymity,

protecting her. Apart from her boyfriend there doesn't seem to be anyone else who might recognize her. Ms K again changes places with her boyfriend so that his back is turned towards her once again.

After the meal, the woman plays cards with the married couple and their daughter. The married couple tell the journalist their life-story. The journalist parries their questions. Ms K can hear this. The woman does not reveal that she has children or mention her status as a grandmother for she looks younger than the other woman even though she must be the older of the two. The younger woman's eyes are full of mute enquiry and consternation. As if to reassure herself, she keeps glancing at her family, who were at least there even if they weren't particularly exciting.

The woman does not stay until midnight when the champagne corks pop. And soon after Ms K also leaves the hotel restaurant with her boyfriend. Up in their room they listen to the Chancellor's New Year speech.

— I wouldn't mind knowing the country he's talking about, Ms K says.

The next day the woman journalist is leaving early. She has to pay an extra day, having originally intended to stay longer. She's already at the reception desk with her cheque when a family man comes up to pay, as he is leaving too. He is dealt with first, which he finds quite proper too. Her turn comes round at last and she is finally allowed to leave the place. Unlike the family man enthusiastically seen off by the hotelkeeper, this time the two parties remain frosty.

Ms K watches her out of the window as she drives away in her car. She has put her arms round her boyfriend's neck and he, standing in front of her, is pressed closely up against her in the narrow gap between the bed and the window.

TALKING AMONG THEMSELVES

*Aren't there any good stories about childbirth? the pregnant
one asks.*
*— Oh yes, there are, says the one in the middle readily.
Someone called K once wanted to give birth to her baby
singing, the way the Queen of Navarre bore Henry IV. She had
thought it was in her power to at least provide a warm welcome
and that this was something she owed to the child.*

*In hospital, the delivery room was overflowing and after
hours of struggling to continue singing to the child down in the
boiler room where she had been wheeled out of the way, the
tune finally stuck in her throat. Screams emerged instead,
suppressed at first but then growing louder and louder, curdling
the blood of both passers-by on the street and patients lying in
their beds. The midwife listened to her tummy every now and
then and said it would take a long time yet, it being her first
child. The young K asked if she could sit up. But it was not
allowed. Inexperienced as she was, she obeyed and allowed
herself be pushed back onto the pillow. Once the contractions
had started to come at one minute intervals, she spent another
twelve hours in the delivery room, on the middle bed of three,
next to a succession of mothers giving birth to the left and right
of her. In between the screams, that were getting louder and
longer, this young woman repeatedly asked to be allowed to sit
up. She was more relaxed that way, she said, and showed them
what she meant. But now there were two midwives at her
bedside, joined for some of the time by three doctors, all looking
at her and whispering among themselves, for it was a difficult*

birth, and none of them allowed her to sit or stand. K pleaded with them, frantically quoting the laws of physics to prove her point. She wanted to have her child with the help of gravity and not against it. By now the woman was screaming in a voice she no longer recognized as her own. She screamed and screamed. She screamed for her mother and finally ended up screaming for a merciful death. Every time she lifted her head, the nurses pushed her down flat on the bed. In the end, they removed her pillow.

About twenty years later, this woman heard that at the time the head obstetrician of that very same clinic had been applying for a national research grant for his work on giving birth in an upright position. It had reached his ears that in some places in the world women were reputed to give birth to their children while standing up or kneeling down. Scientific teams were to be sent to investigate these rumours. For years now research teams had been travelling among the natives in the bush. For after all, the head obstetrician was an influential person and the research funds flowed freely. These teams of young doctors were investigating these persistent rumours of women who give birth standing up although, as soon as the scientists turned up at the places mentioned to them, the women affected not to understand anything and were most unfriendly. Not once was a scientist allowed to be present and witness a woman standing or kneeling to give birth.

But at last one field research team was lucky. Or rather, at last one of them had been successful in arranging the affair by bribing and blackmailing the men. Access to the women giving birth in return for schnaps. At last they could watch an African woman bear her child in a kneeling position and even film the whole thing too.

Back in the clinic, the pillows were still being pulled away from under the women whenever they felt the urge to sit up. And not one of them insisted on sitting up despite all this. For they had never heard of anything like it from their mothers or grandmothers. Each time they felt the urge, it had to be dismissed as one of the vagaries of pregnancy, it wasn't to be taken seriously, not by the doctors and not by the women either. Meanwhile, the head obstetrician was writing scientific reports based on the results of the field research. He learned nothing about the way his own maternity cases were suppressing their instincts. In order to increase the efficiency of his work and to avoid being called out to a birth when it was inconvenient, he was one of the first to introduce the pharmaceutical industry's new drugs to control contractions and it was not long before he started inducing births exclusively on weekdays, to keep the evenings and weekends free — for his family, so he said, but really for his girlfriend and for his scientific articles on upright birth. Women no longer screamed the house down for hours and hours on end, as Ms K had done in her time.

Over the years, the head obstetrician became an internationally recognized expert in his field. He discovered that in medieval Europe women had still been giving birth in a sitting position. He was fond of livening up his scientific articles with the appropriate illustrations. He kept a jealous and spiteful eye on the competition he faced from the growing women's liberation movement in this, his very own province. He surreptitiously procured all the literature coming from this quarter — in all languages he could lay his hands on — and it was not long before the collection to be found in the second row of his library was more encyclopedic than that of any woman. And without admitting as much, he drew enormous profit from all these publications. While the women in his clinic were being given gas and air and giving birth to their children between the hours of nine and five, Monday to Friday, he would be talking shop with some colleague from abroad, discussing the best position for childbirth and praising the squatting position *because it ensures a good supply of blood to the baby's brain. In the past, as in the case of Ms K, lack of oxygen was the cause of numerous complications and post-natal damage to both mother and child here.*

It's already been pointed out that it was only much later that Ms K discovered all this was going on at the same time as she was having her baby. She had never got over the fact that the welcome she wanted to give to her child in this world had been so thoroughly spoilt and she never stopped feeling guilty. At some point, her guilt turned to anger. She could still vividly see how, after twenty hours' labour, the nurses had bundled away the poor little newborn thing without even laying it down beside her, not showing it to her until the next day.

— Would you be so kind as to tell me why you think this story will cheer me up? the pregnant one demanded aggressively and a little anxiously.

— It's supposed to encourage you to not let yourself be bullied and to trust your own feelings. And to encourage me too.

— What she means is there's a practical reason for all our nattering and nattering and talking and chattering and nattering again. It helps prevent mishaps, the third one said.

HALLOWEEN IN BERLIN

Ms K had lost her soul years ago. It occurred to her one day that she might still have a chance to find it again. The chance she was thinking of would owe nothing to the friends she had relied on in the past. She would recover her soul, she thought, or at least she fancied she would, if the man who had stolen it from her would look her straight in the eye.

From the moment she knew this, Ms K started going out again other than when it was absolutely necessary, such as going to work. She went into town again, even passing through areas of the city she had long avoided. She conquered her fears and began shaking hands with people again. Her keen eyes would scan the crowd. Keen, so as to be sure not to miss him.

It was on the eve of the first of November that she dreamt of him. They met in the doorway of a motel. But before he could raise his eyes to hers he had already turned and fled. He ran behind the house. Ms K sped off after him, running towards him from the other side. If only he would meet her eyes just for a second, Ms K implored in her dream. Then, at last, she could become human again and feel. But he veered off in another direction as soon as she turned the corner and caught sight of him. He recognized her by her feet or by the fuss she was making but he didn't look at her. They raced round the house for hours and hours, or so it seemed to her, and when she woke up in the morning, Ms K was exhausted.

She had intended to leave Berlin first thing in the morning and drive to West Germany by car. But now Ms K sat there wrapped in a blanket without stirring. She was waiting. The dream was trying to tell her something. She must have patience and listen carefully until the message came through to her.

The hours passed. It was nearly midday by the time Ms K brushed away the fuzziness of the dream. She stretched and gave a wry grin. It was quite simple. He had not looked at her. He hadn't done it. She would have to remain soulless, one of the zombie squad. She'd almost got used to it by now. There was even something to be said for it. Since she had been in this state, she had come to understand a lot that had been a mystery to her before.

Above everything else, zombies lacked all sense of direction. They no longer shared the same basic concepts of decency and respect and certain other of the seemingly normal conventions of human co-existence. At some point, and this was invariably tied up with someone near and dear to them, they had come to reject decency and respect and thus they slid into a state of soullessness. For a long time Ms K was at a loss as to how she should react to the simplest of situations. She was no longer familiar with the rules of social intercourse. The fact that they had lost all meaning was absolutely typical of her condition. It was a mystery to her why certain rules should be valid and others not. With time, however, she had learnt to process certain items of information in the usual way again, albeit mechanically. If she met someone she knew and the weather was fine, she was again capable of putting on a friendly face and saying what a lovely day it was. Later, she could even juggle around with certain aspects of social life with ease. She was ideally suited for the work she did in all sorts of political campaigns and research groups. For she understood conflict, she never lost her cool and nothing could daunt her. She was dependable. The secret was that she was basically indifferent to whatever it was that she was doing.

She sometimes declared with amusement that it was none other than the zombies who, by virtue of their obtuse ability to sit things out, reduced both national and international deadlock to manageable proportions. She even had a new boyfriend but he was so indifferent to her as a person that he was completely unaware of her condition. She only ever came unstuck when she was faced with children.

Ever since she had become one herself, she recognized the other zombies and they recognized her. There were survivors from Vietnam, from the torture chambers in Chile and concentration camps among them. But they weren't the only ones. There were also relics of private wars and disasters. They had one thing in common. They had not been reduced to their present state by an anonymous enemy, but had invariably been betrayed by friends. They had been crushed by identifiable individuals. There weren't all too many of them as it happens. But sometimes she would come across one of them at a party. This was embarrassing for they tried to keep out of each other's way. These semi-living or soulless individuals needed the presence of real people to learn by imitation or await salvation.

While having a bite to eat, Ms K flicked through a book on Celtic law that she had bought the previous day for an article she was writing. Aimlessly, she read one or two paragraphs. She read how the dead are said to come alive and mingle with the living at Hallowe'en. That's today, she realized. All Saints' Day. It would be a Bank Holiday in West Germany and there would be more traffic on the motorways than usual.

Ms K closed the book. If it hadn't been for that bloody dream she would have got away hours ago. She would even have arrived by now. She made a telephone call and postponed arrangements that she would now no longer be able to keep. Then she sat down again idly. She didn't know what was holding her back but she still couldn't leave yet.

At last, early in the afternoon, she got up.

She would drive off now.

It was a sunny day and exceptionally warm for November. At the border, long queues of cars were waiting at the Griebnitzsee checkpoint. Berliners off on holiday. The sounds of music, voices and laughter wafted out of the open car windows.

A quick glance to check the tyres. It was something she had got into the habit of recently.

People who were accustomed to the procedures of crossing the border had switched off their engines and every few minutes or so they would push their cars a little further towards the passport control and the conveyor belt that transported the travel documents. She had already answered one officer in the negative when asked whether she was carrying any children or firearms. The cars stood in long parallel rows and every now and then the travellers turned their eyes up to heaven in resignation or smiled at each other in amusement at the East German bureaucracy. It was like the 'bowing to the inevitable' attitude that relatives sometimes adopt towards an aunt who has gone dotty. She simply has her quirks and she's not going to get rid of them any more now. They were again asked if they had any 'firearms, ammunition or radio transmitters' and she heard some joker in another car next to her answer, 'Only strategic ones'.

Then she was through customs and driving through the 'Zone'. The more she drove the stretch by car, the more she used this once taboo word. VoPo police checks were positioned behind every bush of any size, lying in wait for speeding offenders and foreign currency. Almost inevitably, a childish game would begin. There were restrictions, but infringements were positively encouraged. Since a great deal of foreign currency was collected this way, it couldn't possibly be in the interests of the authorities for drivers in transit to actually keep to the speed limits. The question was how quickly could you spot what might be a VoPo patrol hideout and slow down in time. Speeding offences had become a sport along the Berlin corridor.

Ms K was annoyed that the good old custom of on-coming traffic flashing a warning to the others had almost died out. She stuck to it rigidly. It would go without saying in Italy, she reflected. Baiting the state authorities was an ancient custom there. The disadvantage of transgressing the law like this was that you had to concentrate on the others all the time. One side was just waiting to catch offenders, and the other side was trying not to get caught. Immersed in thoughts of this kind, she was promptly caught, waved onto the hard shoulder and required to stop.

The tool of the state came up to her window and demanded to see her 'travel documents'. The officer disapprovingly told Ms K that she had been driving at more than the permissible KAYPEEAITCH.

— I beg your pardon, would you repeat that.

The VoPo-man stared at the woman suspiciously. Was she making fun of him? But no, she kept a completely straight face.

— At 117 KAYPEEAITCH.

— But I had to overtake, said Ms K. What else am I supposed to do when the person in front of me is only driving at 98 KAYPEEAITCH? I have to accelerate by a third as much again. You get taught that in every driving lesson. What else was I supposed to do?

— I can't tell you that either, said the officer. But you mustn't let yourself get caught because the speed limit in the German Democratic Republic is 100 KAYPEEAITCH.

No point in quarrelling, no point in flirting. It cost 40 DM and Ms K paid up immediately. But first she had to wait, as part of the punishment. For longer than she had hoped to make up by speeding. To cap it all, she was required to sign that she had paid.

— Me? I won't sign anything. It's you who have to sign to confirm that you have received the money. That's the way it is under capitalism.

The officer refused. He gave her the carbon copy of the receipt. But Ms K wanted the original. Well, she didn't really want it at all, she would have thrown it away immediately, but abstract curiosity made her want to know what would happen next.

The officer glanced over to his colleague and then said he had to make another call. He walked with the other officer to the car in which a third man was waiting. The three men surreptitiously peered out of the window in her direction and pretended to talk the matter over.

— What you're up to is not without its dangers, Ms K reflected.

The VoPo-men had probably come to the conclusion that she was harmless, being a woman. They're right there, thought Ms K.

Let them make a bit of foreign exchange out of me for all I care. At least it's an understandable motive. I can cope with that.

Earnestly and with an air of importance, the first VoPo-man came back again with a copy of the receipt. Ms K again said something about the original, purely as a matter of routine. The VoPo-man replied that it would cost more if she insisted on having the original. Ms K began to admire the sheer affrontery of these bribeable police officers. But she could do without any further argument now. She wanted to push on. She'd had enough of it, she was in a hurry all of a sudden. Leaving the speed check behind her, she immediately accelerated to about 120–130 hoping she wouldn't get caught a second time, and somehow she knew she'd be lucky.

The sun hung over the horizon to the left of her, large and red, as she drove past the Magdeburger Börde service station and saw the car. A lone car, a Citroën, was driving towards the motorway on the access road. It was like being struck by lightning; Ms K knew at once — it's him. The sun was shining onto the car windows with such blinding intensity that she could only just distinguish the make of the car, but she couldn't see what colour it was or who was inside it. She shot past the access road. Looking into her rear view mirror, she saw the car thread its way into the stream of traffic a few hundred metres behind her. It moved straight over to the fast lane, which was forbidden, and was following Ms K. It matched its speed to hers. They were overtaking all the other cars and quite obviously driving along together although there was quite a considerable distance between them. Was it five hundred, a thousand or two thousand metres? Ms K couldn't judge.

The dream.

Was that why Ms K had waited all morning? Was that why she had been stopped by the VoPo, so as to meet up with him here? Could he have known that, when he started tailing the car that was driving along at a speed that suited him, he was driving behind the very person who wasn't really present any more thanks to him? He had classed her as so inferior that it was no longer even necessary for him to observe the usual social conventions. She simply didn't exist as far as he was concerned. She had been blotted out. And now he might be driving along behind her.

Ms K told herself to snap out of it.

That sort of thing just doesn't happen, she told herself. It's stretching things too far, all that VoPo voodoo. But the fear crept up inside her. She felt frightened. It was a long time since she had experienced the feeling. That certainly seemed to indicate that he was somewhere in the vicinity.

If it is him, I must prevent the story ending the way it did in the dream, she thought.

But probably, she comforted herself, she was underestimating the translation of dream into reality. I probably just need a better radio in the car. One that works — to relieve the boredom on these monotonous roads. East Germany is no place for ghosts. There's a difference between Halloween and All Saints' Day. A dream is a dream.

Would she please concentrate and change down a gear, she told herself firmly, trying to snap out of it again. There was a dip in the road ahead and they were bound to be there making another speed check.

She was right. Then she accelerated again to a hundred and thirty. She was glad to see that the Citroën behind her wasn't waved to the side either. The story would appeal to him, she thought.

She lost sight of the car behind her several times as she drove down a hill. But it regularly popped up again in her rear view mirror.

After about thirty kilometres they arrived at the border. As was only right and proper for East Germany, they had to file into lane and change down from a hundred to eighty to sixty to forty to twenty. This meant that the cars coming from behind closed up on those in front and there it was, the car behind Ms K was the self-same Citroën. It was now possible to make out the silhouette of a child on the back seat. The car drew closer and she could see her one-time beloved in the rear view mirror, the very man who had robbed her of her soul and broken her heart. The dream mustn't be repeated, she thought. This must end differently. He must look at me. He must have mercy and look at me. He wasn't looking her way yet. Could it be that he was turning pink? One quick glimpse and he must have grasped the situation. And then he actually managed to avoid looking straight ahead even once in the entire twenty minutes she then spent with her eyes glued to her rear view mirror. He was trapped. Another car rolled up behind him in his lane, there was a fence to the left of him and another line of cars to the right of him, she was in front of him. The ingredients of the scene were such that he could not escape her. She registered the fact with satisfaction. The man nervously lit a cigarette and spoke irritably to the child behind him. The child was jumping up and down on the back seat and, so it seemed, laughing straight at her. But she couldn't bear any distractions now. She was waiting to reunite with her soul. It was bound to happen any minute now. She was waiting for just a glance from him. Every few minutes someone in front of her passed the checkpoint and she drove forward a few metres without looking. She stared into the rear view mirror, waiting for him to look up and their eyes to meet. He was staring blankly to one side or to the child behind him and he too drove his car forwards without looking. Dazed, she told herself she could stop, she didn't have to drive on. She could turn round. But no, that was impossible. It would mean breaking the continuity for a fraction of a second, for that brief moment of blackness between two frames. And she couldn't do that because she was striving to prevent a repetition of the dream and somehow that seemed to mean not letting the man out of sight.

She could faint. She could get out and go up to his window and say, 'Hallo'. She could die on the spot and the border guards could summon him to carry her into the VoPo hut for identification and there they would discover that years back they had travelled together. She remained glued to her seat, still staring. He was the one more likely to faint. He was still pink in the face and was already lighting his second cigarette. It began to dawn on Ms K that, however propitious the circumstances, this story was not going to end the way she wanted.

The story of Death in Samarkand crossed her mind. A man sees Death in Damascus. He is filled with fear and runs home. There, he packs all his belongings and, taking his wife, his children, his camels and servants with him, he rides for three days and three nights until he reaches Samarkand. Before the city walls Death comes to meet him saying that he had been more than surprised to see him in Damascus three days ago since he had long been expecting him here.

Ms K got neck ache from staring in such an uncomfortable position. She knew the face well. It was flabbier than it had been in her day. She didn't feel frightened anymore. She didn't feel anything. She was quite empty. She went on staring. Would she take a second look at him if she were seeing him for the first time today, she asked herself? Would they still be together if they hadn't separated in that awful way? Could they have become a married couple, sitting next to each other in silence? Perhaps they were lucky that everything had turned out the way it was now?

He didn't look up. She was cruelly disappointed. Later, Ms K did the test on other people in cars that had stopped behind hers. She looked at them in the rear view mirror and they looked back at her. It never failed to work.

Now it was her turn to show her passport and transit visa. She drew her hair back for comparison with her passport photo. She had lost. She drove out into no-man's-land. The speed limit there was thirty. Two cars in front of her an overcautious driver was crawling along at twenty. This left a gap between it and the cars in front of it. And into this gap shot her one-time lover, illegally overtaking on the right and without so much as a look to the side. It was dusk and she noticed that the rear light on the nearside wasn't working.

I hope he doesn't get into trouble, she thought.

He now reached the West German checkpoint in front of her. He put his foot down as soon as he left it behind him. He was driving fast, as fast as he could. But her car was faster and she soon caught up with him. She overtook him and looked over to her right. He was clutching the steering wheel, looking straight ahead now. He was afraid of her. Perhaps he was afraid she would provoke an accident. But she wouldn't do that. She didn't want to have to die a zombie. This game was repeated several times with him overtaking her too. It ended up with her being trapped in between two lorries, unable to change lanes because the traffic was too dense. It was completely dark by now. There was no end to the line of cars driving ahead of her. Row upon row of identical lights. The car with the faulty rear light had vanished.

TALKING AMONG THEMSELVES

I've got another one to tell you, said the middle Ms K. But it's not a proper story. It might become one if you want to hear it. It's not particularly funny either. But then again, there might be more to it than you think.

— Go on then, tell us your non-story, said the others benevolently.

— It starts quite normally, she said vaguely.

— Is it long?

— It is both long and short. It depends on who's telling it.

— Make it short.

— A friend of mine asked me to recommend that the work of an orthodox Jew be subsidized by an institution in which I have some influence although the work he was doing was only peripherally related to the aims and objectives of the institution.

I would have had to wangle quite a bit for it even to have been accepted as an application. But there were other reasons for my not wanting to push it through and I wanted to discuss these with my friend but he wouldn't hear any of it.

— Is that it?

— The broad outlines of it.

— Did you have a row?

— We didn't let it get that far.

— Did the man get his money then?

— He didn't even apply.

— Who's the story about, the Jew or your friend?

— It's about me not being able to break free, said Ms K with a diffident smile. And about friendship. But in a way it's about

Soviet-Polish relations too. To cut it short, the question is: How can a small country succeed in achieving autonomous relations with a superpower? It's also about 'Bitburg' and the 'History Debate', she said with a crooked grin, although of course we'll never be given a hearing at the round-table conferences unless we're wearing a tie. It's about what I experience as violence, but also about what I see as my weakness. But even violence and weakness are just the tips of an iceberg.

— That's a hell of a lot all at once.

— So there's no structure to the story?

— I wouldn't say that. In fact, the outlines are very clear. But as far as I know they've never been put into words before. They're what you might call circuitous.

— Well, you can tell us the facts for a start. Where, when, what, how? What did he say? And what did you say?

A TELEPHONE CONVERSATION WITH A FRIEND

Ms K was just about to leave the house at midday, when she thought of making a long-distance call to her friend A to tell him that the money he had lent her was on its way back to his account. He had sent her a considerable amount, immediately and unhesitatingly, without any guarantee of ever getting it back and without kicking up a fuss about it being tied up in stocks and shares. In that way he had been different from others who she had approached earlier because they had more money. She could have told dozens of stories like that about him.

She dialled his number and he was in. He was delighted to hear from her and they were exchanging notes about this and that when it occurred to him that now he in turn could ask for Ms K's assistance on behalf of someone else. He told her the story of an orthodox Jew who was in need of a little more money to be able to complete some research that was relatively far advanced. He asked Ms K to put in a word for this man at an institute to which she belonged. Ms K said that, in principle, there was nothing to rule out supporting work of this kind but that it did not exactly fit in with the aims of the institute. Quite irrespective of the quality of the work, which would obviously have to be assessed, she had misgivings on two counts. First, that kind of support would open even more doors to collusion, and there was enough of that already. And secondly she had a personal prejudice against orthodox Jews. She hastened to follow this with an explanation, trying in vain to prevent it sounding like a justification.

The destructive will in the Five Books of Moses, she said, had already brought enough evil upon mankind over the last few thousand years, poisoning and perverting people's minds. The literally murderous patriarchalism of the Old Testament, the intolerance, the contempt of women, the intellectual taboos, the submissiveness to authority and the ideology of extermination they contained were informed with the same spirit, often phrased in the same words, as the ideology of those who had murdered the Jews. Take Iran, for example, before and after, she added, with more than a hint of defiance. At any rate, supporting Jewish orthodoxy would not be expressing the way she personally came to terms with her past as a German. But this was just her spontaneous reaction, shorthand so to speak. She did not wish to put paid to anything in a hurry right now on the telephone without knowing more about it. She could be wrong after all. She didn't even know what his friend meant by orthodoxy. So she would suggest that the man present his work, and send in a formal application. It could be discussed then. However, a crucial question as far as she was concerned was whether the modest funds of the institute were not better employed in assisting those whose lives were at stake today.

At this point, Ms K's friend interrupted her. 'We', he said sharply, were responsible for the destruction of one race, not for the others. Ms K impatiently cut him short saying that this was a bureaucratic figure of speech. He was over-simplifying the matter. She couldn't accept the 'we'. She hadn't had any part in it. They had other responsibilities these days if he would just be kind enough to allow her to recall Iran, Cambodia, the nuclear question and Seveso, not forgetting Uganda and the destructive potential of armaments. These places might almost all be further away than Dachau was at the time but, after all, distances shrank in this day and age of mass media and, consequently, they bore equal responsibility for the crimes associated with these places. Their voices had suddenly assumed a metallic ring which took Ms K back to the days when she and her friend had held diverging views about Lenin, the Kronstadt sailors and the aims of the women's liberation movement. Discussions of that kind had usually ended with him slamming doors in fury and her knocking at his door again days later, to his immense relief.

Ms K immediately felt guilty. There she was complicating things again. She suddenly resented the fact that he had approached her with this matter rather than one of the men at the institute. Apart from her, they were all men there anyway. It would probably have taken them no time to reach an agreement. They would have had a pleasant chat man to man, she thought tensely and hoped that she wasn't over-interpreting things. The men would have discussed the technicalities of awarding the grant and managed to perform a politically commendable act into the bargain, publicly presenting themselves as friends of the Jews.

Ms K suppressed a rising sense of irritation and reasonably pointed out, even if it were with a lump in her throat, that it would be setting a precedent to grant this kind of subsidy. All the others could equally justifiably come along and claim a right to subsidy — the gypsies, the Eritreans, people seeking asylum. They might as well close the place down if it came to that. As it was, their resources were barely sufficient to give a handful of people the chance to explore a few things more thoroughly. And if it were at all possible to support anyone financially, she could also name a number of women's projects that were doing essential work of precisely this nature and had received absolutely no support from anyone yet.

Swallowing some of his anger, her friend replied that 'women's' — and here he paused for a fraction of a second only to continue with a totally inept and absurd expression –

'pet issues' didn't interest him any more. She got the impression that he had only just managed to stop himself from saying 'women's shit' or 'women's crap'. He had just steered clear of a monstrous insult and toned it down to a more acceptable one. Hardly changing their tone of friendly politeness, they brought their conversation to a rather abrupt conclusion before it came to the all too familiar slamming of doors.

The tears were already pouring down her face as Ms K pressed the elevator button and she was still crying as she drove to her meeting. She pulled herself together when she arrived, late and her mind otherwise occupied. The others were already wondering where she had got to. She was so furious with herself and with him she felt weak. She needed the strength of a horse to endure this day after day, which she had, thanks to her weight training. The merest suspicion of doubt at his words and love was lost. It's not as if it's a crime to ask who 'we' is, Ms K hissed, justifying herself. It's not a crime to ask what is important and what isn't if funds are limited. The telephone call had had the effect of forcing her to face up to reality — she had to be weak if she wanted to enjoy warmth and affection. She had to bow and scrape if she wanted to be hugged. There was a long line that stretched from father to man to man, with a sliding scale of sanctions for independence. She had thought that less nagging meant love.

Ms K was not a particularly timid person. But it was a fact that it took courage for her to hold views that differed from those of her friend. There was no supposedly Free West for her to emigrate to where they were just waiting to hear her views. Her impudence was not that she had views of her own but that she wanted to have them discussed. Punishment for this was immediate. Twenty years of women's liberation had now made it possible for a colleague to ask her, as a colleague, to do them a favour. But she still had no right to expect anyone to contend with her right to hold differing views. Indeed, Ms K was not even sure that what she felt really did boil down to a differing view at all. That was precisely what she would have liked to work out with him. She wished she could talk to her friend and jump from one thing to another, changing the topic at will without any rules or regulations. In a sense it was her own fault that he became insulting at the end of their telephone conversation. After all, she could have kept her mouth shut. That would have been what he wanted. He probably wasn't even aware of how insulting he had been. That was another aspect of this non-story. She should have answered back:- So that's how it is, you're not interested in these women's issues! Well, I got sick and tired of your Jewish issues long ago, I'm fed up to the back teeth with your precious race issues not to mention the perpetual issues of nuclear power and South Africa.

Realistically, Ms K reflected that she didn't even expect him to be the one to want to pick up the threads of their unfinished conversation. He would be giving her the biggest surprise of her life if he did. A worst-case scenario atomic megablast, so to speak. But she could probably eliminate this possibility sooner than the nuclear power lobby could that of a meltdown. She loved him and couldn't break free of him. So she would wait for a chance to waylay him and force him into this exchange. An act of love that would merely be another act of aggression in his eyes. She wondered what the world would be like if these catastrophes weren't passed on and discussed everywhere with friends and sisters and mothers and aunts. If the telephone stopped buzzing every day and women stopped telling each other what he had said and what they had replied. How explosive do you think the mixture would be without these safety valves?

Whatever happened, the first step towards reconciliation always came from her. There was method in it. She hated it.

Didn't it occur to him? Didn't it ever strike him? Was it
beneath his dignity? Did this lovable person quite uncon-
sciously take it for granted that she should give in without
caring about anything else? He was genuinely delighted every
time she responded. He was visibly relieved. But he himself
never took the first step. He didn't aim to humiliate her. He
just did.

— From a materialistic or materialized point of view, Ms K
said, now speaking to an imaginary audience for she was
rehearsing the speech she was going to make him, her friend's
unconscious yen for conformity led, for instance, to the
memorials to the victims of terrorist regimes that are in all our
towns and cities. Every single one of these abject stereotyped
figures had bowed heads and sloping shoulders. Whether in
marble, granite or metal, they all publicly proclaimed the
conditions that have to be met before a person can enjoy the
regard, sympathy and concern of others. All traces of joy,
merriment or defiance must be erased, for a start. Anything
that suggests unpleasantness or a sense of danger, indeed
anything that suggests individuality altogether. As if only
pitiable and helpless creatures had been exterminated and no
honest and upright people, no children or singers or dancers
or flirts or farmer's wives, no nauseous characters or
exploiters, no power-seekers or men with muscles. According
to this logic, a person has to hang on the Cross first and then
he or she would be worshipped. She wouldn't go along with
that.

In all friendship, that was the limit as far as her desire for
equal rights was concerned. She was convinced that he could
follow her if he would only try and take her seriously for once.
She listened to him, after all. Anyone who had any intelligence
knew that people would face enormous problems, including
psychological ones, if the two German states were to be
reunited after more than forty years of separate politics and

development. When it came down to uniting men and woman after more than five thousand years of hate, persecution, murder, mutilation and the destruction of ideas and knowledge, it was suddenly supposed to be enough to blather on about partnership to accomplish it. Were they really supposed to have accomplished it just because he emptied the rubbish into the dustbin, put up with her opening her mouth for a change and brought her to orgasm. It was only to be expected that far deeper layers would rise up in revolt. And while we're about it, she had already told him that years, if not decades, ago. She had told him then, overwhelmed by the insight, that EVERYTHING, absolutely EVERYTHING, would have to be reconsidered in a fresh light. If they really wanted to stop tormenting each other and casting aspersions on each other's character, the suppressed ideas of womankind would have to come to the surface first, worldwide. There would be nothing to cling to any more then. He had simply laughed at the time. But it hadn't been encouraging, that laugh.

Ms K reconstructed what they had said. Their phone call ended in stalemate as they were arguing from irreconcilable points of view, which lay beyond the scope of their conversation. As far as he was concerned, the mere fact that she had even thought of supporting a women's project instead of the Jewish project ranked her among those who placed the crimes against the one on a par with the crimes against the other. Under no circumstances would he allow the one to be confused with the other. That was stretching his tolerance too far. It was this conviction that made him utter the words 'women's pet issues'. That was the point where he restored things to their proper proportions. That was the point where he performed what amounted to an act of resistance. That was the point where he was at one with the good Germans for whom forgetting was not something to be got away with cheaply (which was what he automatically accused her of), it was his way of defending himself against his own assumption that her mention of other atrocities detracted from those committed by their own people. That was the accepted doctrine. On that public opinion was firm, or better still, firmly stuck in a rut. The die was cast as far as those who stood on the side of moral impeccability were concerned. With the monotony of a prayer wheel it would be repeated over and over again that the Nazi crimes could not be compared with other crimes. As if suggesting that would automatically imply that the criminals who were still alive should no longer be held accountable for their crimes, that no help should be given to the surviving victims and that a repetition should not be prevented by all available means. Their incomparability was drummed into everyone in such a ritualized manner that to doubt it was practically enough to class the doubters in the same category as the people who had perpetrated the crimes. Their incomparability had apparently been laid down once and for all — by whom? — and had the effect of an intellectual taboo. Ms K had impinged on this intellectual taboo in her brief conversation with her friend.

Ms K worked out which comparisons were taboo. It was taboo to compare the systematic extermination in the German concentration camps with the extermination that took place in the Stalinist camps. It was taboo to compare the extermination in the gas chambers with the extermination of the kulaks or the people slaughtered in Cambodia because they could read and write. Or with those who had been murdered by the Germans earlier in Namibia. Or with those who had been hit by the atom bomb in Hiroshima and Nagasaki. Or with the Africans whose feet were amputated because they were larger than the feet of another tribe that had risen to power after having been oppressed itself. Or with My Lai. Or with the wiping out of the Armenians. Or with those who had been put to death on the wheel by the Church.

Or with those who had been hung, drawn and quartered. Or with those who had been burned alive by the Church. It was taboo to compare the torturers in Uruguay with the Nazi torturers. The Iranian Revolutionary Guards with Hitler's SA. It was taboo to compare the random extermination of mankind that is technically possible today with the bureaucratic extermination of the Jews.

Why exactly was it taboo to make these comparisons? What were the real reasons? Horror at what had become technically feasible? Ms K discovered that she was unable to rank the atrocities in hierarchical order. She noted down Eichmann's statement that a thousand corpses were statistics and next to it she wrote down the statement that had been broadcast by several radio and TV news programmes and repeated over and over again without one of the newsreaders faltering for a second:

> "The foreign ministers of the two superpowers met in Geneva for joint discussions on how to minimize the risk of accidentally launching an atomic war."

That was what she would have liked to discuss with her friend. Eyes that are fixed on the millions, Ms K soliloquized, are really fixed on the fascination of numbers, not on individual people. They saw the huge piles of glasses, the piles of shoes and hair. But you can't count the dead. There's absolutely no sense in it. Mathematics stops there. Woman or man, it's the individual that is destroyed. That's why it makes sense to take a personal interest in at least one individual man or woman. Many may experience death simultaneously but it's always each person's own individual terror, their own stomach that turns, their own bowels that open in horror. It made no sense whatsoever to the dead to speculate about what was ghastlier, to be drawn and quartered by the Church,

to be tortured first and then burnt at the stake, to be gassed by
the Nazis, or to be shot by the Stalinists while doing forced
labour. People who refuse to acknowledge that this kind of
horror must start somewhere, that it has to be tried out on a
small scale before it can be carried out on a large scale, only
confirm Eichmann's thesis that a thousand corpses are
statistics. They only see the past in terms of statistics. But if it
were only a matter of statistics and nothing else, Ms K said, it
would be easier to identify the enemies. Whether it was
relevant to life or not. The awful thing was that everyone was
so eager to point their fingers at easily identifiable enemies.
But what about the women who were sent to the concentration camps by their own mothers, what enemy profile were
they supposed to develop? Or take the Jewesses who married
Nazis after the war? What's the implication of saying that
that's statistically irrelevant. The whole point of the exercise
of coming to terms with the past, Ms K said with disgust, is
apportioning the guilt, not preventing a repetition. The Nazis
had the one priceless advantage that their rule was limited,
that they were on the losing side and that their victims were
called Jews to simplify matters statistically. The gypsies,
communists, homosexuals, tramps and others had to fight to
be mentioned here at all. If we're going to talk about horrors,
then about all of them, if you please, and not only about the
ones that are statistically significant. This was her own
personal contribution towards coming to terms with the past.
One had to differentiate between what was harrowing for
those who had been murdered and what was harrowing for
those that survived. In the face of the new weapons of mass
destruction she found it impossible to be amazed that the
Nazis had also used the latest technology available for
extermination. Today, we didn't need enemies or people to do
the sorting, to process the horror with semi-trained skill.
Today, we could dispense with the Auschwitz chimney

stacks. We could have people vaporized. No, Ms K found it impossible to gauge who suffered more, a Chilean woman subjected to electric shock torture on her genitals or a gypsy sent to the gas chamber. And it was for this reason that she would probably have voted to support people who were suffering today.

Ms K would have loved to be able to discuss with her friend whether the authorities' tacit agreement about the uniqueness of the crimes was not just one big hoax. Would it be paying less respect to the victims if people who were alive today opened their eyes to the enormity of man's capacity to commit crimes? Did the people who wanted to prevent this really in all earnest believe that a sorrow shared is a sorrow halved? Her friend was an intelligent man and Ms K wanted to talk it all over with him. She wanted to weigh up the pros and cons with him and and look at the problem from all angles. After all, he was the one who had taught her to check everything twice over. She would have liked to have worked out with him whether the point of this formula, if carried to its logical conclusion, did not in fact amount to covering up the crimes of the past as well as those that were in the making today. In this way, the historical winners, who had no less blood on their hands than the Nazis, could continue to neglect any mention of their own doings. This was the real reason behind the ban on comparing one with the other and, all in all, a perfect example of brainwashing.

But emotionally, she continued, still speaking to the wall, she, Ms K, felt the need to do something to commemorate the roughly thirty million people (yes, 30 million, since numbers are so important) who, according to scientists' calculations, forcibly lost their lives during the colonization of America. No one had ever done that. And she would also like to see the hundreds of thousands, if not millions, of people who had been burnt as heretics and witches included in this

commemorative act. Allowing for the fact that the world
population was far lower centuries ago — and she was only
following the traditional line of argument here — these
figures weren't exactly insignificant either. But why get all
worked up about Bitburg when the Pope was able to travel the
world without there being a public outcry at the crimes of his
institution? What she was trying to say was that there was a
long story behind her being so sensitive to the expression
'women's pet issues'. Yes, it made her feel bitter, Ms K said,
when self-righteous morons showered scorn and contempt
over those who today claimed they did not set out as twenty-
year-old SS and SA men to murder Jews but to create a
national socialism, and then rambled on about living in the
country. But the same self-righteous morons would see
nothing wrong with the churches setting up peace groups here
and now even though these self-same churches were still
sticky with the blood of the colonized, the heretics and
witches she had already mentioned, and, in their very
organization, continued the tradition of these priestly mass
murderers. It was a phenomenon that existed side by side
with their atrocities just as the 'good' motorways built by the
Nazis existed side by side with the bad SS.

So if her friend was going to go on about 'our' guilt as he
did, would he please be so kind as to explain to her where it
began and where it ended. How many centuries will it take for
it to come under the statute of limitation? When would it be
permissible to talk about 'Jewish pet issues' with the same
impunity as it seems already possible to talk about 'women's
pet issues'? Exactly how many years would it take to figure
out the difference between 'our' crimes and the crimes of
times immemorial? After all, neither you, my friend, nor I, K,
had any part in any of them.

Ms K believed that the dead of times immemorial still
haunted the present awaiting redemption. What was the

magic number that transformed 'inhuman' crimes into normal ones? That would allow later generations to sleep in peace and no longer forced politicians to keep mentioning them in order to set themselves apart?

It would have been her dream come true, Ms K reflected, still sobbing, if he had simply asked her: OK, what does orthodoxy mean to you then?

She would have had no difficulty in forming her thoughts then. She hated butting in without being asked. It made her seem like a know-all. It made it impossible for her to talk about her own uncertainties. And so they found themselves in the depths of barbarism.

The three Ms K were now spending their last evening in the hut.

Their conversation was interspersed with long intervals and pauses for thought. They ate and drank and packed their bags.

— Why did we laugh at the story about 'giving birth lying down'?

— It had something to tell us? But what?

— They dictate the conditions. They do the deciding, said the pregnant one.

You have to fit in even if it's no longer so obvious to others that we do. HE dictates whether you sit or lie down, who is healthy and who is ill. Who deserves affection and who doesn't. Whose the weekends are and whose the weekdays. Who gets fucked, how long it takes, who gets paid for it and who gets a cuddle for it. Who has a social right to sympathy. Who has to waste their energy in fear that something might have happened to him when he doesn't ring, that he might have lost all interest or found someone else. He does the defining.

— Which HE?

— The archetypal HE.

— And if he doesn't do the defining and choosing, then, my dear, there's something wrong with your superHE.

— We're controlled by this superHE.

— You don't have to waste your energies on HIM. You can leave, can't you.

— That's just it. Leave. It's always the same. Even we are

*doing it. Away with whatever it is you don't like. Away with
your past, into the dustbin with it. Knock off their heads, off
with their pricks, 'away with'. On all levels, right up to total
annihilation. We haven't got a chance.*
— *I know stories in which decisions aren't made, Ms K said
emphatically.*
— *Tell us.*
— *A woman was living together with a man who went away on
business to another town for three days a week and didn't want
her to visit him there. He had rational grounds for this and, for
a long time, they seemed plausible to her. But one day she
wanted to give him a surprise. She could no longer bear the
strict separation of one life from the other.*

*Without suspecting anything untoward, the woman entered
a fully furnished flat only to find there another woman who
imagined herself and her life, her very happy life with this man,
to be the genuine article and, of course, she knew nothing about
the other woman either. They sat down together on the sofa
waiting for the man to return and confronted him with their
knowledge.*

*Both women left the man and they became firm friends.
Neither of them could stand his cowardice.*
— *I know a woman who has two boyfriends. She's afraid of
losing the first and can't leave the second. She doesn't know
what's going to come of it. But she has made clear what she
wants. She's not deciding who deserves an explanation and who
doesn't. She's taking a risk. It's wearing for them all.*
— *Women tell lies too.*
— *But how did the story of the two women on the sofa end?*
— *Neither of them found a new man, the older woman laughed.*
— *They regretted their courage later.*
— *It's more than a prick can take.*

*They all looked at the pregnant woman's belly again,
thinking it might be a son. A sweet little son. But how on earth*

could they love and support him, and what men, in what part of the world and of what colour, would there be to set an example to this son-to-be?

FOUR WOMEN AND A MAN

One of the women was a biologist, then there was a politician, a personal secretary and singer. They had all reached the top in their field. At some time each of them had, in an hour of reflection, resolved to do all they could wherever they could to weaken the patriarchy, men's society, what was left of the *schützenfest* or whatever it was they happened to call their exclusive gatherings. It was in pursuit of this aim that they had all got to know and admire one another, partly by chance and partly by design. They had, as it were, sniffed at and recognized each other for what they were. The few women who reach the top of the ladder notice women colleagues in other fields and make a mental note of them. They were all four familiar with the crooked practices involved and did not flinch from using them if required.

One fine Friday evening the four of them met at a grand hotel in the Aosta valley which was housing a high-level congress and various smaller conferences simultaneously. That all four of them should meet up there was — as far as the biologist and personal secretary were aware — pure coincidence. The politician had managed to rearrange an appointment to be there and the personal secretary had arranged for the singer to be flown in specially to perform in the exclusive evening show. There was a problem that the women desperately needed to discuss in detail and they were all hard pressed to fit in another appointment.

Later, they became acquainted with a fifth woman at the hotel who had specialized in marrying rich men and pocketing a handsome alimony settlement in the divorce proceedings that would follow. With the money thus earned, she would act as a mysterious and anonymous patron for various projects which, as the politician had discovered, were invariably initiated by women, though they might not always be carried out by them, and invariably resulted in opening the door for other women to enter new areas of influence. All four had resolved to draw her more firmly into their circle once they had settled their own problem. Incidentally, it was customary for the four not to discuss any of their individual enterprises. Only occasionally would they come across something that seemed to point to one of the others. This gave them a sense of satisfaction every time. The biologist, for instance, saw to it that the facts about genetic research did not remain secret but could be placed under the control of the public at large and had up to now managed to do so successfully without her name being publicly mentioned in this connection. By way of a third country, the politician cultivated private contacts with a high-ranking woman politician from the Eastern Bloc to prepare the ground for women politicians to conduct secret inter-Bloc negotiations on the problems of patriarchal rule and armaments that were strategically just as important as the Geneva disarmament talks.

The personal secretary had become extremely skilful at letting dissatisfied industrialists' wives in on the secrets of their husbands' exploits in exchange for information. The exploits aroused the private curiosity of the wives and the information served to untangle certain intricacies in the world of multinational trade relations and related scandals. The singer, who travelled around a lot and got to know personally all the people whom the others met in their professional capacities, was also in a position to throw in a lot of useful tips. The cheese that had been smelly for so long was slowly becoming riddled with holes. It would never have occurred to any of the gentlemen importantly hurrying to and fro carrying their guaranteed genuine leather company briefcases and with their plastic name badges pinned to their shirts — it was hot and dress was informal — that this meeting-place had been arranged long ago and specially selected by the four women now drinking cocktails by the swimming pool.

Individually, each of the women marvelled time and again — they never discussed it among themselves — that they could conduct their business relatively openly. Of course they were careful for it was evident that they were under the observation of various agencies and at some risk. Probably no one got wise to their game because they did not use men's tactics to perform their acts of sabotage. Two women who had been put onto the politician by the Secret Service had so obviously been trained by men that she recognized them at once. The politician played cat and mouse with them for a time and then turned them around. One of them subsequently worked as a double agent for a while, the other left and retired from the job for good.

So there they were, four smart professionals sitting in their deckchairs and allowing their glasses to be filled with swimming pool cocktails. They waved to their male colleagues and members of the boards and managing directors who would so dearly have loved to keep them company and amiably but saucily shooed off a handful of photographers after they had approvingly made eyes at a handsome camera assistant who blushed at their stares.

They took care to keep up their image of looking sexy, intelligent and a bit casual. This added to their charm and yet made them appear all the more harmless.

They returned to the problem that had brought them there.

For there was a blot on their reputation that united them. As women so high up in the hierarchy, they ran short of men to escort them. That meant that they arrived at too many of their numerous official engagements unaccompanied. However, if they wished to continue working successfully, which they most certainly did, they had at all costs to avoid creating the impression of loneliness. Women who created this impression were as stigmatized as if they were suffering from a skin disease. The problem was either that the men were intimidated by their success or they felt themselves to be inferior or that the women's lovers affairs were such that they were not presentable in public. It had on a few occasions been discreetly pointed out to the personal secretary that her love life was her personal affair, after all people were more broadminded nowadays, but couldn't she have a little more regard for the reputation of the company they were in. This was in reference to the embarrassing incident when the company director had suddenly found himself on a par with a temporary messenger boy at an evening reception. The personal secretary skilfully retaliated by saying that the messenger boy in question was not only that but also a student who wanted to learn the business and work his way from the bottom up. Nevertheless, she could only afford that kind of thing once, that much was obvious. Certainly, the directors moved in quite different circles as far as their love lives were concerned, but then they did not bring them along to company receptions. That was exactly why they had wives. The foursome had no such opposite number.

They had to change the complexion of their solo appearances, but how? Money was no object for any of them. They could even afford to invest a little in an experiment. Nor did they lack courage. The singer came up with the idea of employing a young man as an occasional escort for all four of them. They all laughed at the thought to begin with but they soon warmed to the idea.

They weighed up the practical advantages. None of them

needed him every day. They all worked in such different fields that they wouldn't be getting in each others' way. A paid escort wouldn't have to have his ego boosted day after day. (Let's hope not, said the singer.)

The personal secretary worked out what it would cost. The young man was to be well-paid and provided with an excellent wardrobe. To reduce their individual expenses — the numerous flights would be the major cost — the personal secretary proposed that the young man should always travel at company or government expense. There must be some way they could claim tax relief. The politician had misgivings, over which a dispute of some length ensued. But the others maintained that these expenses were by no means too much to demand of the taxpayers. It wasn't fraud for they were all engaged in essential peace work and they needed the escort in order to be able to pursue it further. Set against the billions the taxpayers had to pay anyway for armaments (without having first been asked if they wanted to), the costs for the young man were negligible and perfectly justifiable. Besides, it was quite normal for men to travel with a companion and a man in their position could always take his wife along with him and declare her against taxes. These arguments sufficed to convince the politician too and so they decided to arrange for the young man — somehow it went without saying that it had to be a *young* man — to fly at company or government expense, even for short journeys.

They worked on the principle that each of them should be entitled to him once a week. They fetched their diaries and divided up the much sought-after weekends and other days equitably. Agreement was reached when their dates clashed. It was only natural that such prominent women fixed their appointments long in advance, and in next to no time the man was booked up for the next three months. The women closed their diaries with satisfaction, their ears red with excitement.

Then they had to come back down to earth — they hadn't found the man yet.

He ran straight into the singer the next day as she was taking a walk. He was jogging towards her and pulled up sharply because he recognized her. He looked ravishing, exuded an eroticism combined with a certain old-fashioned innocence and was his late twenties. The singer asked him to sit down with her on the grass. He told her that he was under contract to run several times a week advertising a mineral water and to enter competitions too. He was under a certain obligation to win and, what's more, he often did for which he received a large bonus each time. He found the job rather boring by now though. He could speak several languages, was a qualified teacher but he didn't want to teach for the time being, had a polite manner and was, politically speaking, an amiable anarchist.

The others observed him discreetly and were delighted to give their OK. The women had decided that it would be better if they did not all meet him together there. Their private lives did not concern him and they agreed, rather reluctantly after having seen him, that they should do their utmost to avoid sleeping with him so as not to jeopardize their friendship with one another. The singer was the contact person, she informed him of the duties desired of him and described the job very matter-of-factly. The young man willingly agreed to his terms of employment. He didn't let on that he had already seen the politician and the singer together.

His employment raised the women's spirits beyond measure and they enjoyed working again. For despite all their professional success they still often lost heart. When they began their subversive activities they had still been relatively optimistic as far as the effectiveness of their work was concerned. But this optimism had wilted after a few years. Their intimate knowledge in so many different fields meant that they were far better informed than the rest of the population and they no longer believed they could change anything for the better, let alone actually forestall a catastrophe by enlightening the public. In fact, each one of them secretly believed that the day would come when the power that they were still striving to achieve on behalf of their sex might even be pressed into their hands gratis once it became known that there would soon be nothing but rubble to govern. Then, women would suddenly be the sole saviours but there would be nothing left to save. They had persevered all the same. They pursued their sabotage without illusions. It was hard work. The young man brought fresh vigour to the cause.

He at once proved to be an exceedingly pleasant and intelligent person and whoever happened to be going out with him was envied. Contrary to the foursome's plans, he attracted more attention than intended. It wasn't that the women's spheres overlapped, but he was a feast to the eyes of the photographers and they soon registered the fact that he regularly turned up at the side of different women. Women, whose interest in him was by no means professional, noticed this too. He could hardly escape the many invitations that were meant for him personally. The four looked on with mixed feelings but held back. They didn't want to prejudice his prospects.

Naturally the young man also had a girlfriend and she was not one to be trifled with.

He was hardly at home any more at the weekends. He went zooming round half of Europe, and the States too on occasions. He promised his girlfriend to reveal all but asked her to have patience for a while longer. He did tell her the broad outlines of his duties but his girlfriend was still so young that his accounts remained confused in her mind and she could make neither head nor tail of them. Clever as she was, she found out about an appointment to which he had to

drive by car. She hitchhiked after him. She even got hold of a
ticket to an excruciatingly boring opera performance.
Looking down from the gallery, she could see him at the front
in the second row of the stalls next to a woman politician she
recognized from the newspapers and next to a number of
other people whom she thought she knew too. She was able to
see how at one point he took the woman's hand in his. Other
people who were sitting behind them could see it too, for one
woman drew her husband's attention to the fact with a nod of
her head. For the girlfriend, a world collapsed.

During the interval, he saw her in the foyer just as she had
caught sight of him and was rushing towards him. He was
familiar with her tantrums and wished to act loyally to both
women. He seized his girlfriend's arm before she could say
anything but then didn't know what to do next. The woman
politician grasped the situation at a glance and seized her
other arm. There was no time to lose so she decided on shock
treatment to subdue the girl and render her speechless.

— If you shut up and don't scream he'll come back. You'll
understand what he's doing at my side soon enough, you silly
girl.

The girl felt both impressed and intimidated by the woman
at the side of her beloved. She was so much older and so much
more self-assured than herself. She suddenly felt inferior.
What was more, she hadn't the faintest idea what was going
on.

— Don't worry, your blue-eyed boy will come back to you,
the politician repeated, and you'll delight in him as you've
never done before.

At this the young woman was overcome with jealousy
again. Her suspicions had been right. Despite the best of
intentions he had already slept with two of the women, or
rather, two of the four had already slept with him. He wasn't a
good lover to begin with but he learnt fast and his young

girlfriend immediately understood what this meant.

Following this incident, the women ended their experiment prematurely. The three months were almost over, as an escort he had been a success, the blot on the women's reputation had been erased for a while, but the affairs, about which the other two women had their suspicions, poisoned the atmosphere. This they wanted to avoid.

And so it was, and was to remain, a delightful episode. For equity's sake and by way of a farewell the other two also slept with him. The young man married his girlfriend and all four women came to the wedding. Later they became godmothers to the twins that soon appeared. As for themselves, the women were alone again, but he had won four friends for life.

GLOSSARY

Berum, Dalum, Esterwegen, Bergen, Moorhausen, Sand-bostel were all concentration camps, administered by the Ministry of Justice rather than the SS.

Bitburg: In 1985, Chancellor Kohl and President Reagan visited the Bitburg cemetery to commemorate victims of the Second World War. The visit was controversial as members of the Waffen-SS also lie buried there.

Maidanek was a concentration camp near Llublin.

Republic of Salo: On 15 September 1943, Hitler freed Mussolini from prison and set him up as a puppet dictator of the Italian Social Republic.

Schützenfest: A local fair incorporating the annual Rifle Club competition.

Venus von Willendorf: A realistic stone age statuette with accentuated sex characteristics.